PSYCHOPOMP & CIRCUMSTANCE

Also by Eden Royce

NOVELS

Root Magic

Conjure Island

The Creepening of Dogwood House

NOVELLAS

Hollow Tongue

SHORT STORY COLLECTIONS

Who Lost, I Found

PSYCHOPOMP

&

CIRCUMSTANCE

EDEN ROYCE

T O R
D O T
C O M

Tor Publishing Group
New York

PSYCHOPOMP & CIRCUMSTANCE

Copyright © 2025 by Eden Royce

A Tordotcom Book
Published by Tom Doherty Associates / Tor Publishing Group
120 Broadway
New York, NY 10271

www.torpublishinggroup.com

Tor® is a registered trademark of Macmillan Publishing Group, LLC.

EU Representative: Macmillan Publishers Ireland Ltd, 1st Floor,
The Liffey Trust Centre, 117–126 Sheriff Street Upper, Dublin 1, DO1 YC43

Library of Congress Cataloging-in-Publication Data

Names: Royce, Eden, author.
Title: Psychopomp & circumstance / Eden Royce.
Other titles: Psychopomp and circumstance
Description: First edition. | New York : Tordotcom/Tor
Publishing Group, 2025.
Identifiers: LCCN 2024034377 | ISBN 9781250330963 (hardcover) |
ISBN 9781250330970 (ebook)
Subjects: LCGFT: Gothic fiction. | Fantasy fiction. | Novels.
Classification: LCC PS3618.O8954 P79 2025 |
DDC 813/.6—dc23/eng/20240729
LC record available at https://lccn.loc.gov/2024034377

Our books may be purchased in bulk for specialty retail/wholesale, literacy, corporate/premium, educational, and subscription box use. Please contact MacmillanSpecialMarkets@macmillan.com.

First Edition: 2025

Printed in the United States of America

10 9 8 7 6 5 4 3 2 1

To my grandma,
who knew how to plan for endings
and beginnings

Strange, strange indeed, these things to us appear
And yet we know they must be right;
And though your body sleeps, your soul has passed
Beyond the night.

—Angelina Weld Grimké,
"To Joseph Lee"

PSYCHOPOMP & CIRCUMSTANCE

ONE

Her final cotillion was in full swing and Phaedra St. Margaret was vex.

Oh, not because of the event itself; no, that was lovely. The location was stunning: a grand ballroom on the top floor of one of New Charleston's mansions, windows thrown wide, overlooking the harbor. The Brockingtons had spared no expense this night, going so far as to hire a smattering of dark-cloaked conjurers. While Phee was not usually partial to magic, finding the excessive ceremony expended to craft such moments exhausting to observe, it did not rankle her here.

The conjurers nestled in one corner of the room, blending in with the shadows as they whispered and gestured dramatically, creating the hovering spheres of light that illuminated and enhanced the varying shades of brown of the revelers in attendance. A lion-footed table stood at the far end of the ballroom, laden with food and glittering crystal bowls, the punch inside seeping a cooling fog that drew the overheated dancers from the polished hardwood floor to sip the fruity, boozy nectar like silk-draped hummingbirds. It was a sight to behold.

No. Phaedra's feathers were ruffled because she was here at all. Her mother's doing, of course. She was of age and unmarried, so this was her duty as a daughter of the Reconstruction. Find a suitable husband, have children, and raise them to carry on the family name and its legacy of enriching the city with wealth and knowledge. The war had ended and she was looking forward to the Juneteenth celebrations again this year to commemorate the end of enslavement for her brethren and sistren. But this dolling up in dresses she would never wear again, and torturing her hair into a dressed showpiece more suitable as a topping for a cake than a hairstyle, was for the birds.

With the edge of her closed fan, Phee flicked aside one of the hovering spheres of light and proceeded deeper into the ballroom. Thankfully, this was the final year she would have to bother with this excessive ceremony. The arrangement she'd made with her mother was that she would attend each cotillion—making an effort to smile and dance and chatter amiably—until she turned twenty-one. By then, she would either be married or resigned to consider suitors below her station, as she would no longer be in the ingénue category. Or, to her mother's unending horror . . . find work.

That was just fine with Phee. She would rather work at her father's distillery than pander to the tender sensibilities of the men who frequented these balls, while succinctly yet modestly enumerating the qualities she possessed that would make her an appropriate lifemate. She had done so every year since she was of age—aside from the few years the war had prevented such events—and she was tired to her very marrow of it.

Just inside the ballroom, Phee nodded at an acquaintance she recognized from an earlier dance and complimented the girl on her dress, receiving one in turn. While she gracefully accepted the kind words, Phee knew the peach-hued silk favored her dark skin and the lace detailing sat perfectly on her shoulders. For all her division with her overbearing mother, she had to admit the woman had good taste and was always aware of the current style. It was her own mother who had taken notice there was no need for the women in their family to wear the cumbersome bustles beneath their gowns to add fullness when their own natural anatomy provided the same silhouette without the padded undergarment. The weather was too hot for all of that extra. Soon other women with nature's endowment followed suit.

Phee swept deeper into the room, her fan clutched in one hand while she made a beeline for the refreshments table. She'd feel better with a drink in the other. As was usual, the refreshment table was surrounded. While she waited her turn, absently fanning her face and neck, Phee caught a snip of stage-whispered conversation between two older women as they left the table with their drinks.

"How long has it been?"

"Oh, I don't know. Five and some-odd years?"

"Can you imagine? And she was from such a good family."

"Her niece is supposed to be here tonight. She's twenty-one already! And still can't secure herself a husband. What grown woman can't manage to hold on to a man? I can't understand it."

"What's wrong with her?"

Their voices faded as they sauntered off to half-heartedly perform their chaperone duties. Phee's heart burned in her chest and heat climbed the column of her neck. They were talking about her, of course, a footnote in the gossip about Auntie Cleo. Somehow, it was still a topic after all these years. Several more people left the table with their potables and the line crept forward. Phee advanced as well, the flicks of her fan doing little to cool her rising irritation. Did they have nothing better to do at a party? Maybe perform their assigned duties? She could see couples getting closer than was seemly and even pairing off to steal away into the darkened balconies overlooking the floating gardens, heady with the perfume of full-moon-blooming brugmansia.

Maybe Papa should accept that invitation to join the Freedman's Bureau; having a position like that in addition to his own business would elevate his standing in the community more and lessen the sniping about her aunt. She let out a weary sigh. No, in truth, it wouldn't. Even her own family sniped about Auntie Cleo, why wouldn't the rest of New Charleston?

When Phee glanced over at the chaperone table, the women were still in conversation. They tittered, heads together like lock-horned rams. She was desperate to know

4

the rest of the vitriol they spat. This was her final season and Phee wouldn't have to endure these parties any longer, so she could say her piece to the nosy Nellies before she and her skirts went scrooping out the doors for the final time.

Her fan hid the scoff that erupted from her lips. If she did tell those women about themselves, the news of her actions would spread like wildfire. Speaking so boldly could easily garner a visit from a doctor to see what was wrong with her mind that would cause her to take leave of it. Especially a gently bred society woman like herself who should know better. Someone would send a winged messenger the instant she turned on her heel to leave and, not having to travel on the constantly flooded roads, the creature would reach the asylum long before her carriage could return to Rosemount. Having her sanity brought into question was enough to put her off the idea. If she managed to avoid the institutions, she'd have to write a plethora of apology notes to the Brockingtons and their guests in order to show her face in town again. No one wanted that.

She blew out a breath as she flexed her feet in the shoes that were just snug enough to keep a body alert with discomfort. The music changed from a jaunty, quick-tempo song to a more languorous one as Phee reached the refreshments and plucked up one of the punch cups. The mist on its surface chilled her as she sipped, thinking of how to approach the matter with the scandal-mongers, when a voice spoke to her.

"Why, Phaedra . . . you've come. I told Mother you would."

Suppressing her irritation, she smiled at the speaker. "Desmond. Yes, I have."

"I trust you are well."

"Thank you, I am. I hope you are."

To no one's surprise, Desmond Sweet fell into step with Phee as she walked away from the refreshments table. He had asked around about her, she knew, but so far she had managed to avoid dancing with him at these soirées. While outwardly mannered, he was said to be a cruel tyrant if one challenged his whims. Only a few long-suffering individuals remained in his employ, and despite his attempts, he had not managed to secure a suitable marriage with a woman of his choosing. Of the two engagements he'd attempted, one young woman had quickly thereafter married another man, and the other young woman's father spirited her away in the middle of the night to parts unknown and had never returned to the city. Phee had been distracted with her thoughts and had allowed him to catch her unaware.

"I think it's high time we've had a dance, don't you?"

Timing could not have been more against her. "No, I don't think—"

She tried to move around him, but he was having none of it. He seized her wrist in an iron grip, and in her shock, Phee released the crystal cup, watching horrified as it fell to the floor and shattered into a million rice-sized grains.

While the revelers on the dance floor and those near the musicians did not hear, the group gathered around the refreshments table paused in their own conversations to look at what had caused the faux pas.

"You are ruining my glove," Phee hissed at Desmond's face as she tried to tug her wrist free, bewildered now that eyes were on them.

The threat of her property ruined had no effect on him. "Soon I will join my father's medical practice. I can buy you more."

"No, thank you. I have more than enough pairs." When her words did not garner her freedom or the intervention of any so-called chaperones, she gritted her teeth. "Fine, then—we will dance."

"I think," he said, as Phee marched them toward the dance floor, "that I am supposed to lead."

"Lead me over there, then." Phee indicated the chaperones with a nod of her head.

Smug satisfaction crept over his face as he took her fan hand in his. The other he pressed to her waist. Instead of the acceptable light touch, his hand lay heavily on her person and Phee shifted her hip to inform him. He acknowledged her discomfort with an unrepentant grin. The desire to miss a step just to stomp on his foot welled up inside her, threatening to spill over.

As they moved through the dance, Phee caught portions of the women's conversation and her suspicions were confirmed. Her aunt didn't deserve to be the brunt of such gossip after what Phee knew was closer to ten years. Ten years . . . Mercy, when was the last time she'd heard from Auntie Cleo?

They corresponded via letter fairly often, especially now that she was of age and her mother no longer intercepted her post. But for the life of her, she couldn't recall the most recent letter. How long had it been?

Phee needed to visit her aunt. As a girl, she'd promised herself she would take time to call in person as soon as she was out from under her mother's purview, but now she was one and twenty, and she still hadn't kept that promise. What had prevented her? Too much of her time spent dodging her mother's wishes and extricating herself from the detailed plans her mother had for her only child's life. While simultaneously making her own plans to push against the unflagging tide of her mother's will, subtly enough to where her actions wouldn't bring down harsh consequences.

And where had all that effort gotten her? She looked into Desmond's reptilian face. He held her too tightly still, and inside her gloves, her hands felt trapped, slick with perspiration. The song ended and she stepped back, applauding the excellent music. When Desmond reached for her again, Phee rapped him smartly on his knuckles with the edge of her closed fan. Before he could recover, she marched away to speak to the Brockingtons and thank them for their generous hospitality.

Tomorrow, she promised herself, nothing would prevent her from making arrangements to visit her aunt. No matter what her mother thought of the black sheep of their family.

TWO

When the tyefrin messenger delivered the notice of Aunt Cleo's death to the house the next morning, Phee's mother praised the Eternal Magician. Then she laughed.

Phee was aghast. "Mother, Auntie Cleo is dead. Some respect, please?"

"Since when did your aunt have respect for me?" her mother sniffed, affronted. She patted her halo of coils, her lip curling. "Always wanting what I have."

For a moment, Phee was stunned into silence. How could her aunt be gone? Only last night she'd promised to visit and now . . . Her blood slowed inside her body, thickening to honey, then crystallizing—immobilizing her. She stared at her mother while warm sunlight filtered through the open door and onto the high ceiling of the foyer, glancing off the chandelier to make a pattern of elongated dewdrops on the cream coffee–colored walls surrounding her.

According to family stories, Aunt Cleo was once babysitting Phee and decided to take her out in the stroller to the park. A few people had gathered around baby Phee to say how adorable she was, and Aunt Cleo had supposedly cuddled the child and said, "I could steal her, she's so sweet." A lady in Mama's social group, out getting some fresh air, had overheard and told Mama, who confronted her sister. Counting on her fingers, Mama had enumerated what her sister had tried to take from her, including Phee's father. At no time did it matter that he had courted Aunt Cleo first. Once Phenton met Madelyn, his choice was made.

Slowly, Phee turned back to the messenger. The tyefrin's face was impassive, but she noticed its eyes—a startling citrine with inky vertical pupils—darted between her and her mother. Best to ignore her for now. Mama, like Aunt Cleo—and like herself, too, she supposed—could be stubborn. Phee turned back to the well-dressed tyefrin.

"Please, continue."

The messenger on the front porch lifted its curved beak in acknowledgment. Its scales, green tipped with gold, glistened in early morning sunrays. Sheer, membranous wings folded along the creature's squat, ridged back, reaching almost to the thick tail it had curled around its small, clawed feet. They were beautiful, intelligent creatures, well suited for carrying messages and avoiding the dangerously slick cobblestoned streets of New Charleston.

"Who will pomp this newly dead?"

Clearly, the messenger expected a swift response. It seemed surprised when Phee's mother shook her head, lifted the hem of her skirt above her bare feet, and stepped backward. She tried to pull her daughter with her, but Phee shook off her hold, rearranged her dress sleeve. The fabric crumpled easily, a hallmark of wealth her mother loved.

"Mother!" she scolded. "She was your sister. Why won't you be responsible?"

"If she were still welcome in this house, I would. There is no reason we— Phaedra!"

But Phee had already held her hand out to the messenger to receive the duty of planning for the dead. She swallowed hard before saying, "I will pomp for her."

"What are you doing?" Her mother slapped her hand away but Phee had spoken the words, opened her palm; the deed was done.

"You have no idea what's involved in planning a homegoing service. The work involved. All those funerary directors descending on you at once, strutting for your attention. It's like being courted by swathes of suitors—only more elaborate and more competent." Her mother cut her eyes at Phee. "Not that you'd know anything about that."

Phee ignored the jick; she was used to her mother's comments about her lack of life partner. "I'm happy to learn, Mother. I've always wanted to work and learn to do things, but you've never wanted me to."

"Where is the sense you were born with? This is not the time to learn, child. You've legally accepted the pomp. If you don't complete it, they will throw you *under* that jail. And not even money or favors could get you out of serving your time."

"I would not abandon a duty, Mother. That's not like

me at all." Piqued at the implication she would toss away the homegoing planning when it became difficult, Phee raised her chin. "I *am* a St. Margaret."

"You won't be so uppity after six months of watery grits and no sunshine, I'll bet." Her mother sighed as she dramatically shook out a wrinkle in her dress. "I should have had more children."

Phee pressed her lips together before speaking. "Perhaps you should have."

When her mother touched Phee's shoulder, her tone softened. "I've done these services before, and you're just not up to all of that, dear heart. It's draining and you get little recognition."

There was the lie. Even as sheltered as Phee was, she knew a well-planned homegoing service gained the planner plenty of recognition, praise from the town government and its people, and in some instances, even brought job offers that could lead to financial independence. Mama's comment had her believing for a moment she was worried her daughter had taken on an impossible task for someone unused to celebrating the life of the dead. A part of Phee had hoped Mama would relent and go with her to Aunt Cleo's anyway. Wasn't that what death was supposed to do? Bring people together? But the lie had fallen so easily from her lips.

And Phee knew the reason. Mama wouldn't want her to successfully complete a pomp because she wouldn't want her only child to thrive elsewhere on her own. She had to control the family. Cousins, aunts, uncles . . . all of their visits for holidays, funerals, weddings, and other special events had to go through Mama. Gift giving was under her purview as well: who pleased her during the year would be treated with lush extravagance on their day of birth and those who hadn't . . . well, they could try again for the following year.

Phee shook her head and motioned for the messenger to carry on.

The tyefrin cleared its throat, beginning the missive again in an elegantly croaky voice, giving her aunt's name, title, location, and date of death. It handed Phee a scroll, rolled tight and tied with a long blade of saltgrass. The fragrance of fine, handcrafted paper and kettle-brewed ink lulled her, and she had to suppress the desire to hold the scroll under her nose and take a deep sniff.

The tyefrin shifted from scaled foot to scaled foot, uncomfortable. "Shall I send a carriage for you?"

"Tomorrow after first meal will be fine." Phee ignored her mother's gasp, and smiled at the messenger. "Is there anything else I must do?"

The messenger looked happy to be released. It recorded her name in a small book that it tucked into an elaborately trimmed jacket pocket. "A carriage will arrive after first meal and take you to the decedent's home."

"My thanks. A moment, if you will." Phee moved to take a few coins from the dish on the foyer table, kept there for exactly this purpose. Messengers had such difficult jobs. People tended to blame them for the bad news they carried. Phee didn't have work, except what she forced her father to allow her to do for his distillery, which was a little book-keeping, and she taught a class on traditional paper-making on the rare occasion anyone was interested.

Domestic tasks that would position Phee to eventually become the partner of some well-bred professional were all her mother allowed under her roof. The only ones Phee could stand were gardening (it got her out of the house), reading (she loved learning new things, especially things her mother didn't approve of), and cooking (she'd be able to feed herself if she ever got the opportunity to leave Rosemount Manor).

The messenger demurred. "Bereaved need not pay for my service, gentle one. My sympathies to you." With that wish, it retreated down the stairs, claws clicking, taking to the air as soon as it was clear of the overhanging porch.

Once the front door closed, Phee's mother lit into her.

"Who do you think you are? You don't make decisions in this house." Her mother sucked her teeth, her stormy gaze flicking over her daughter as if she were wondering where she'd gone wrong. "What will you look like—traipsing over to that ridiculous city she owned?"

Through sheer force of will, Phee avoided rolling her eyes. "She didn't *own* it, Mama. She founded it. And she's your sister!" Phee quieted her voice, so as not to anger her mother further, though she suspected that was impossible. "I don't even know what it's like to have a sibling—but I couldn't leave her there alone for the city to do who knows what with."

"Why not? She didn't take you when she left."

"I'm sure you wouldn't have let her if she wanted to."

"Watch yourself, Phaedra." Mama peered closely into Phee's face—similar to the way she had when Phee was a little girl and needed to learn a life lesson. "You don't know a thing about that place where she lived. The businesses there—florists, cemeteries, undertakers . . . especially the undertakers."

She stood eye-to-eye with her daughter. "You have no idea if they'll do decent work. What are you going to say when people ask who did the body?" She scoffed. "That is, if anyone decides to pay their respects."

"How could you not attend your own sister's funeral? That's just cruel."

"Think that's cruel after what Cleo did to me? To this family?" Madelyn Simons-St. Margaret's back stiffened. "I will not help you at all, not financially or otherwise. Not one coin."

Big words from her mother, who was usually willing to throw coins at any problem to make it go away. Phee kept her voice calm, even though she was shaking inside. She'd never gone against her mother's wishes before. Not to this life-altering extent. But someone in this family—the one that shaped her aunt, then forced her to leave—had to care.

"I understand that, Mother. And I'll use the money I've saved."

"You'd better." Her eyes narrowed while she paced in a tight circle in front of her daughter. "Well, this is the most foolish thing I've ever seen you do. Why can't you see the best thing for you is to marry Desmond? I guess since you're grown now, you don't care about my opinion anymore."

Marry Desmond? Phee suppressed a shudder. She'd rather pull her own teeth. "I do care, but—"

Her mother stopped pacing and clapped her hands in front of Phee's face to punctuate her words. "You. Can't. Pomp. For. Anyone."

While the words stung, Phee put starch in her own back, held her head up high. "I'm doing this, Mama."

Hands now on her hips, her mother glared at her. "So I see. And I'm going to let you fail at it so you can bring your uppity rass back here ready to listen for once."

For once? More like for a hundred thousand times Phee did as she was told without questioning, without talking back, without speaking her heart. A hundred thousand rough-edged pills she'd swallowed in order to keep peace, to show respect for her parents and their sacrifices to raise a daughter worthy of the St. Margaret name. The ghosts of her mother's past words visited her now. *She had the opportunity to make something of herself in this age. Why was she fighting against it? Didn't she know her ancestors had lived enslaved for centuries?* She knew, she knew. Phee's throat was rubbed raw from the times she'd swallowed her opinions; her face ached from holding her tongue. A vision-shrinking throb lived behind her right eye, accompanied by a crushing pressure in her cheek and jaw.

Phee's mother stomped away as best she could in her bare feet, likely to find her father and complain about how their only daughter had gone rogue. As she stood alone in the

foyer, listening to her mother's footsteps retreat, Phee fretted. Maybe Mama was right—she had attended homegoings, but only the wake on the night before and the
service on burial day. She had no idea of what went into
planning the entire ceremony.

However, she couldn't think about that now. She had
to pack. Phee lifted the hem of her skirt and dashed upstairs to her bedroom. Tomorrow, she would start proving
she could do something on her own, without her father's
money or her mother's pushing, instead of waiting for
someone to see her worth and marry her. She was going to
lay her aunt, and hopefully the bad blood flowing through
the family, to rest.

THREE

A hatbox of her aunt's letters had residence in Phee's chifforobe. She drew it out, loosened the ribbon tie, and set the lid aside. She drew out the latest letter she'd received from her aunt, dated almost a year ago. It was written on the stationery Phee had created and given to her as a birthday gift several years before.

7ᵗʰ of May, 1867

My Dearest Phaedra,

I find such joy in your letters. Delightful to hear you are keeping up your mathematics by taking on the bookkeeping. It is a shame your father only allows you to check the work he has already done and set aside. Still, it is keeping your mind sharp.

But tell me more of what you are doing—what else occupies your mind and heart? Music, sculpture, animal care? Are you taking long walks to inspire a bit of verse? Tell me all that is happening and I will encourage you on any pursuit you choose.

My garden is blooming and lush, and I often have a

friend over for luncheon when I have time to even sit down during the day. The city is bustling now, and the many new residents who have found my little town need my assistance. After the war, so many have lost their homes. Speaking of the war, you wrote to me last of the state courting your father to join as one of the heads of the Freedman's Bureau. I am certain he will be in good company there.

I must let you go now—there is much to do. Awaiting faithfully your next letter.

Love you madly,
Aunt Cleo

Phee read the brief letter again, stroking the fine grain of the paper while wondering why she hadn't noticed that another letter had not followed. In addition, she wondered why her aunt had said her father would be in good company with the Freedman's Bureau. She ordinarily did not mention him or Mama at all. Nevertheless, it was an error on her aunt's part. Only this year had the papers reported gross "mistakes and blunders" within the organization that in many ways made the situation worse for the freed people. It was horrible knowledge to possess, but her father would never have allowed any misuse of finances. The workings of her father's distillery ran like a tight ship.

She folded the letter and returned it to the box. Aunt Cleo had adamantly refused her offer of money when Phee mentioned it in a letter once. Her response had been so swift and brusque that Phee never broached the subject again. How had she let all those years pass without a single visit? To see if her protests against the offered funds were due to pride or if she truly was content? She knew how: all of her energies were spent artfully dodging her mother's attempts to shape and mold her life. It was only now that she wondered if her mother's unfailing efforts to keep her aunt exiled from the family had hit their mark with such accuracy that Phee's plans had fallen apart without her own notice.

No more. Phee returned the letter to the hatbox, the hatbox to the chifforobe, and her attention to packing. After including an appropriate black dress for the funeral service, she folded a pair of her father's old trousers that she'd plucked from obscurity and tucked them under a fold in the dress. The trousers were in the case should she need to handle something awkwardly achieved in her skirts. Now to gather two blouses and two skirts, and all the needed underpinnings. There was no telling how long she would be away.

Later that evening, a knock on her bedroom door startled Phee out of her drifting thoughts of what was to come. Her father stood in the doorway with a silver tray, a cloche-covered plate in the middle.

"Hungry?" he asked.

"Starving."

"Thought so."

He strode in and placed the tray on her vanity table. On someone else, his long legs and arms might look gangly, but Phenton St. Margaret managed to avoid awkwardness in his movements. He folded himself onto the edge of her bed to lean against one of the four posters, while Phee moved to her vanity, lifted the cloche. The rich, wafting scent made her stomach growl.

"Cheese grits soufflé!" she gasped. "My favorite!"

"I know."

Phee lifted her spoon to dig in. "I didn't know you knew how to make these."

"I didn't. Your mother did."

"You sure it isn't poisoned?" After a moment of consideration, the scent of smoked cheddar wafted past her nostrils again, and Phee decided she didn't care. She spooned a bite into her mouth and huffed out a pleased breath.

"If it were, you'd be in trouble." Her father chuckled a moment before sobering. "Your mother loves you, Phee. We both do. She only wants what's best for you."

She gazed up at the ceiling—a way of distancing herself from the inevitable attempt to dissuade her from pursuing a path she'd chosen. Not this time. "And what is best for me is not taking responsibility for Aunt Cleo?"

"A lot happened between your mother and her sister. Old history that never got sorted out." He shook out a white linen napkin and placed it on his daughter's lap.

"And now it never will be."

He sighed. "No, it won't."

"Why is she so angry? It's only a homegoing service."

"You know that isn't true." He removed his spectacles, rubbed his eyes, slipped them back on. "This is the final show of care. A huge undertaking—no pun meant or intended. You've never planned a service before. It's a lot to do."

"In school, event planning was one of my best subjects. The fundraiser to build new lodgings for students who have to board in the girls' dormitory was my idea. And it was successful. Plus, I'm organized and focused. I reorganized your ledgers and—"

"I know, but this is different." He patted her knee in a gesture made to comfort, but it had the opposite effect—making her feel more childlike and incapable. "It's also the emotional toll it takes on a person. Going through their things, finding out their life, figuring out how to say goodbye. You won't want to endure the presentations of all those morticians, vying for the honor of laying your aunt to rest."

Her father sucked in a lungful of air through his wide nose, then blew it out. "Not the least of all, it's big business and they can put on some pretty inflated productions. So many important decisions need to be made. You'll have the eyes of the whole town on you."

The spoon paused halfway to her mouth. "Do you think I'd get my head turned by some fancy song and dance and not choose the best person? Or that I would break down under the weight of responsibility and not be able to make a decision?"

His eyes widened, owl-like. He blinked, then rocked back and forth on the edge of the bed, choosing his words. "Of course not, Sugarfoot. But you've never done a settin' up, either. It's the hardest part."

Phee ate more of the soufflé. It melted on her tongue, leaving a faint creamy smokiness. This was the most her father had spoken at one time in all the years she'd known him. He tended to be a quiet man, speaking only when he'd had enough of Mama's constant haughty chatter.

If Phee were honest with herself, she'd admit she hadn't thought of any personal toll. Hadn't thought of anything, really, except that her aunt was a member of the family and deserved to have family send her off. If that meant sitting up all night with her body before her burial, then she'd happily do it. She was surprised her father hadn't nudged her mother to go along with Phee's decision and give her aunt this final send-off. Every other time she wanted to venture out on her own, the subject of family was bandied about. *Family is everything, Phaedra.*

She'd always liked her aunt when she was growing up. The woman had been bright-eyed and full of life, loath to conform, and full of stories. Phee had wanted to be like her. She bit back a sigh. *Time in the river . . .*

"What did she do, Pop?" Phee asked. "What was so wrong that Mama is ready to let Auntie go to the ground without as much as a song?"

He crossed one long leg over the other, clasped his fingers around his knee. "She . . . ah, stole something from your mother."

Phee put down her spoon and the scraped-clean ramekin, patted her lips with the napkin, then pushed away from her vanity and sat next to her father. "Stole what?"

"A necklace of your grandmother's. An heirloom. Your

gran was to be laid to rest in it, but sometime during the settin' up, it disappeared. We found it in your aunt's bag. So, the whole family just . . . We asked her to leave."

"That doesn't sound like her at all." Phee frowned. Her aunt was so open-handed, the idea of her taking instead of giving was unthinkable.

Her father shook his head. "I mean, it was such an awful time. We were grieving. People do strange things when they're deep in grief."

In a flash of memory, Phee recalled shouting and raised voices during her grandmother's homegoing service. All the family, both her mother's and father's sides, had been there. They were congregated, listening and watching the sisters argue. Phee had been what—ten, eleven?

Her father had approached them, and for a moment Aunt Cleo's face lost some of its righteous anger. Then her father placed his arm around her mother and asked her aunt to leave. Auntie Cleo glanced at the faces gathered, none of them understanding, none accepting. Phee had run to her and hugged her waist, wailing when Mama yanked her away by the arm.

Auntie Cleo had looked right at Mama when she said, "You are a liar." She lifted the hem of her dress and crouched down to Phee's height. Phee tried to go to her, hot tears blinding her, but Mama held fast, both hands clutching her daughter's narrow shoulders, her sharp little nails biting down. "Love you madly, Phee."

After a flurry of hasty packing, Auntie Cleo was gone. After a few breaths, Mama made some flip comment and the rest of the family chuckled, pleased the tension was broken. Friendly chatter resumed, and Mama headed off to the kitchen to refill the evening buffet. Pop had excused Phee and let her head upstairs for the rest of the night to cry and do her own mourning. That was the last time she remembered seeing her aunt.

"She's family," Phee said, putting her hand on top of one of his larger, browner ones. "I'd hate to think if I did something the family couldn't forgive me for in life, that I'd be relegated to having the city look after me in death."

"I understand, honey." He looked unsure for a moment, then his heartening smile was back. "I thought you might say that, so here's something for your trip." He brought out a wooden box and presented it to her.

When she opened the lid, a long-necked glass bottle lay inside on a pile of fragrant oak shavings. "Agricole? This is from your private collection."

"I know."

"It takes you years to age this. It's—"

"For you. This is the first time you'll be away from home, and doing a task this important. I thought you might need a sip now and then."

"Thank you." Phee hugged him, feeling his thin frame through a layer of starched cotton. "Are you sure you can't come with me?"

"No, I'd like to stay married, thank you."

"Even to keep your only daughter out of the cold, un-forgiving confines of jail?"

He rubbed his chin thoughtfully. "Perhaps I could be

persuaded if a certain only daughter could find it in her heart to accept a particular doctor-in-training into her favor. The Sweets are a fine family."

Phee adjusted one of the pins in her hair. "Jail it is, then. I hope you'll visit."

They laughed, then Phenton stood to leave. He took the silver tray, kissed his daughter's forehead, and headed toward the door.

"Pop, couldn't you reason with Mama before she threw Auntie out of the family?"

He pressed his lips together a moment. "There's no reasoning with your mother when her mind's solid. I hope someone comes to the settin' up."

Phaedra nodded, knowing no one in the family would dare defy Mama and show up to help her. The weight of the duty she'd taken on tugged at her shoulders. She squared them and went back to packing for the trip. "I do, too."

FOUR

The next morning, Phee sat on the porch with her bags at her feet, waiting for her carriage to arrive. She squinted in the bright sunlight to watch the sprinkling of rain falling on the eternally flooded streets. Elders used to say that phenomenon—rainfall while the sun shone—meant the devil was beating his wife behind closed doors. It was an uncomfortably frequent occurrence, if true. She really hoped the devil's wife would leave him soon. No one should take that kind of abuse.

She shifted on the porch swing and nudged herself into a slow rock with one booted foot. But what kind of abuse should one take? None, presumably. Phee thought of her mother's harsh words when she had accepted the pomp for Aunt Cleo and wondered if the woman's actions yesterday or this morning had been the worse experience.

Breakfast with her parents had been an uncomfortable affair, silent save for the occasional clink of silverware against china plates. At first, Phee had tried to keep up mild and pleasant conversation over the creamy coddled egg and toasted rice bread. Her mother's refusal to respond paired with her father's painful-to-watch attempts to toe a line between the two women made her give up the effort. Instead, she focused on spearing the sliced fruit in her bowl with her fork, knowing her mother preferred her to spoon it up. Her mother's lips tightened but still, she didn't correct her, and Phee considered it a tiny victory.

At first the light breakfast had settled her stomach, but now the meal bubbled in her belly. Her tremulous nerves, or was it excitement? Both warred within her, the opportunity to make an impact in one family member's death as well as the opposition she faced from another's disapproval. Once she got in the carriage and was on her way, surely the nerves from the latter would fade.

A hippocampi-drawn carriage approached; the pair of creatures with their elegant front legs and strong back tail fins navigating the waters with a familiar clip-slosh rhythm. Phee leaped to her feet, swung open the front door, and stuck her head inside.

"Mama, Pop! I'm going—the carriage is here!"

There was no response. Her father was probably working in his home office in the cellar and too far away for Phee's voice to travel. Mama likely heard her just fine but was sulking in that haughty way of hers. There was, however, a small sweetgrass hamper of food that had been placed inside the door. Ruefully, she picked it up. At least Mama didn't want her to starve.

Phee looked to the road; the carriage had pulled up. The driver was about to step from it onto the narrow esplanade raised above the water level to allow people to walk throughout New Charleston without getting their shoes and hems wet. She glanced around the empty foyer again before reaching into the drawer of the side table and removing a folded piece of paper. Phee tucked it into her satchel, draped her jacket across her arm, then smiled at the carriage driver as he stepped from the esplanade onto the porch steps and gestured to her bags.

"Shall I store these for you, miss?"

The day was bright and Phee shaded her eyes with her hand to see him better.

"Please," she replied with a heavier heart than she'd expected at the lack of send-off. "I'm eager to be on our way."

Once inside the cool, darkened interior of the carriage Phee relaxed, pressing her back against the padded seat. After the brightness of the sun, it was a relief to be out from under its scrutiny. She closed her eyes, basking in the dimness, until she heard the driver speak to her.

"Pace, miss?"

"I'm sorry?"

"The pace you'd like to travel, miss. Haste or leisure?"

Secured in the recess of the carriage, already her nerves had begun to abate. She touched the basket of food gently with one foot. There was no need to rush to get there. Even if it took most of the day, it didn't matter.

"Leisure, please." She leaned her head back and closed her eyes.

The gentle rocking of the carriage lulled Phee into a calm she hadn't felt only minutes ago. As the miles passed, the burn of her mother's fury eased enough for her to justify it into maternal concern. Regardless of that, Phee was a grown woman now and it was high time she stopped letting events occur around her and began taking up the reins of her own life. Desmond wasn't essential in securing her future. She could do that herself, and accepting this pomp was the first step. She would put together the perfect send-off for Aunt Cleo, one that showed her love and in some small way made up for not being there while her aunt still lived. If all went well, perhaps Phee could point to it as experience to secure employment. If the news of the homegoing would reach New Charleston, surely one of the local funeral directors would hire her on.

Phee removed the document she'd taken from the drawer in her parents' house, a triple-fold parchment-colored bond paper, and lifted the shade on the carriage window enough to read the funeral program from her grandmother's service. It was from Manning's, the only funerians ever allowed to touch the bodies of well-to-do Colored people after death. The raised ink of the ornate script shimmered in the sunlight:

*The Order for the Guidance of the Eternal Light
Within Sister Charitha Simons Toward Home*

This was the level of pomp expected for members of her family. Phee read over the order of service slowly, three times. Processional, poem, call and response, invocation, eulogy prayer, testimonies. And the music—so many songs . . .

Worry fluttered in her throat like a trapped June bug. This duty was more than she'd expected. It wasn't only managing not to fall asleep at the settin' up. With a pot of tea or coffee she could manage that simply. It was bearing Auntie Cleo's eternal disappointment of not having the send-off she deserved. It was letting down the hopes of an entire town who she suspected had their own ideas of how to lay their founder to rest. Her mother's angry words returned to her over the clip-slosh rhythm of the 'campi's front hooves and back fins. *What are you going to say when people ask who did the body?*

Yes, she had attended her grandmother's service, but she'd been a young girl. The age where your help wasn't needed during the times you wanted to contribute the most. She'd spent most of the preparation time at school or in her room, sent there by some distant adult relative who didn't want to field her questions and suggestions. Even her sharp-edged memory of Aunt Cleo leaving that fateful evening had dulled.

The planning of and preparation for the service had been a mystery to her, but she'd crept to the top of the stairs and overheard a lively discussion of music choice and which soloist should perform. Whether a poem or a psalm should be read was too much to decide, and one of each made it onto the program. The extended service, along with a eulogy delivered by a dismal man with a monotonous voice, almost put young Phee to sleep. Mama had planted her sharp elbow into Phee's side as she was about to drift off.

At the settin' up, there had been food—masses of it—that had fed the family for days while they stayed at Rosemount, eating, drinking, playing cards, and telling stories. It was during this revelry the day before the interment they had discovered Aunt Cleo's mistake. Mistake or deception? It had to be a mistake or an act of grief, because no one would ever steal from the family like that, would they?

Love you madly, Phee.

Eager to be rid of the memory, Phee turned her gaze from the past to the present rolling by outside the carriage window. Rain had been falling for the past hour, and the clear floodwaters had changed to an opaque murk. She shielded her gaze from the reflection of the sun off the standing water and allowed the gentle pace to lull her into a doze.

Abbot, the driver, stopped around noon at a way station, allowing her to get out onto a narrow, covered platform to stay dry. The floodwaters had receded some now they were out of the city. Phee stretched her legs while Abbot, in a wide-brimmed hat, his trousers tucked into knee boots, led away the pair of dappled gray hippocampi that had been coupled to the carriage since morning. 'Campi were fine for the flooded streets of New Charleston, but as carriages left the city for drier climes, they were unsuitable. He soon returned with two sleek bay horses that he hooked up in their stead. These large, noble creatures were perfectly built for traveling the roads ahead since the rain had slacked to a light but steady drizzle.

On the bench seat next to her, Phee set out a jar of mixed pickled vegetables, assorted crackers, and spicy benne-seed spread, along with a few soft wheat biscuits, salted honey butter, and scuppernong jelly. A handkerchief with her mother's initials embroidered on it lay at the bottom of the basket. Phee opened it to reveal a handful of waxed paper–wrapped peanut candies. Her favorite. A soft smile formed and she rewrapped the handkerchief, tucking the treats into her bag for later. When she offered Abbot to share her meal, he shyly accepted, taking a small amount of the food, then retreating to lean against a supporting pillar of the way station's platform. Out of the rain but a respectable distance from his client.

Phee watched the rain as they ate. "Have you ever arranged a homegoing, Abbot?"

"No, miss. Lot stronger people in my family to do that." He shrugged and bit a pickled baby carrot with awkward but surprising delicacy.

"It's difficult to imagine a person stronger than you, Abbot." Even with his stooped posture, he was a physically large man, with broad-knuckled hands.

"Strength in the mind, miss. To deal with arranging and things, all while your own heart broke. Don't know I got that in me." He brushed crumbs off his hands and leaned up off the pillar. "Thank the Magician my wife is strong where I ain't so much."

"I'm glad to hear you have made a good match, Abbot."

There were no other patrons at the way station. Even the stationmaster himself was putting up a sign he was taking luncheon. It was peaceful here, sitting under cover while watching and listening to the rain slack up. The bays seemed to be enjoying themselves, snorting to each other while pulling up mouthfuls of grass to chew.

Alone but not. This space Abbot had given her while still being present was blissful. Phee smoothed back a coil of hair that had become puffy with the moisture in the air and laughed to herself, letting her mind wander a bit. Picturing herself as a benevolent queen of a castle was a particular favorite. As was taking over Pop's business one day. A more distant fantasy was attending the ball once more, not as a guest seeking a suitable marriage, but as a patron of the event. Once all the girls were on the dance floor, she would announce that she had opportunities for employ for each and every one of them, if they so chose. Then she would exit the building, leaving stunned faces and a waft of French perfume in her wake. Behind her, she would hear the shuffle of silk slippers descending the stairs to follow her. She would not look back.

One of the horses whinnied, jolting Phee out of her thoughts. She realized Abbot was waiting for her instruction.

She cleared her throat. "How much longer will we be on the roads until we arrive?"

"If we keep leisurely, 'bout another five hours, miss."

"Well, we'd better get back to it."

Phee packed away the uneaten portions of food into her basket and stood to dust off her traveling skirt. With a sharp nod, she indicated her readiness to resume their journey. Once she'd settled in again, they continued on their way, the gait of the horses bringing a briskness to the journey the 'campi hadn't.

Unable to resist any longer, Phee removed one of the peanut candies from the handkerchief. Since she was a little thing she'd always loved these sweet, salty, chewy treats. She unwrapped one, already anticipating the pleasure of it. Mama made them so rarely, Phee saw it for what it was: the only olive branch her mother felt she could extend. She placed the small square in her mouth and leaned back on the carriage seat. The candy melted slowly, releasing the flavors of roasted sugar cane, vanilla bean, and a touch of sea salt. Phee worked one of the peanuts loose from the candy square and crunched it on her back teeth.

Along with the peanut candy, the gentle rocking of the carriage soothed her. This was her first long trip alone and she wondered if it would have been a good idea to have some company. If she had asked Desmond, he would have accompanied her. She let out an unladylike snort. Eagerly accompanied her, she was sure. Was Desmond such a horrific choice of lifemate? He was from a good family, as her father had oh so casually mentioned, handsome, and full of potential. Rumors of his behavior were just that—rumors. If they'd been said about anyone else, she would have paid them no mind at all. Maybe when she returned home, she would contact him. Extend an invitation for afternoon coffee. As the candy melted away, Phee rallied and sat up.

It felt as though they'd been traveling forever and Phee wondered if it was some juvenile sense of time she held on to where each passing minute in reaching a destination felt like an hour. Abbot had mentioned strength in the mind as necessary for planning a homegoing. Not intelligence, but an ability to endure your own pain while working for the good of another. Phee had confidence in her quickness of mind, but had never had cause to test her mind's strength.

Aside from the schism that parted Aunt Cleo from the family, Phee had not endured many trials in life, and she couldn't help but worry if she would come up short with such an important event. It would be a public embarrassment to the family if she failed, and if she had to run back to Rosemount, her chances of finding a suitable lifemate would be greatly diminished due to the scandal. Phee fanned herself with her right hand, suddenly overwarm. She consulted the watchpin attached to the lapel of her jacket and found time had passed normally and it was her eagerness that dragged out in front of her like the drying road. She attended her posture, straightening her back and lifting her chin. Strength of mind, indeed.

Sunset accompanied her carriage into town, turning the sky and its paintbrush clouds a range of sherbet colors. Through the lowered window, cool air swirled in, heralding dusk's arrival. A wooden sign marked the entrance where the road narrowed into the main drag:

THE MICRONITY OF HORIZON
All are welcome.

Phee dragged in a relieved breath. She was here.

FIVE

Differences between Horizon and home were startling. No silhouettes of tyefrin messengers speckled the skies and no esplanades had been installed above the flooded roads to walk on in order to avoid the wet. The streets themselves were a marvel. Instead of submerged cobblestones or muddied puddles, they were dry and lain over with a smooth black surface people walked directly upon. The surface also amplified the sound of the horses, making the clip-clop of their gait echo around her instead of muffling it as the dirt roads had. Phee winced, resisting the urge to stop up her ears, but her discomfort did not last beneath the onslaught of fascinating newness around her. Far beyond the fears of earlier, she found herself in a state of wonder at the sights around her as the carriage ventured deeper into the town.

Well-lit shopfronts lined the main street, but Phee couldn't see anyone inside. In fact, only a few persons seemed to be out at all, likely due to the dinner hour approaching. A hum of insects greeted her through the window, accompanied by the rush of wind through the well-groomed evergreen trees. Spruce and pine gave the air a freshly cleansed scent. An owl barked out, warning the night creatures it was awake and would be coming soon. All in all, a welcome relief, as for the past eight hours hooves and carriage wheels had been the only distinct sounds.

House styles and sizes varied widely here, but were all well cared for. Some of the windows were lit like the shop-fronts, but Phee couldn't see into them as she passed, despite her attempts to lean forward and peer in. For the privacy of the residents, of course, but her curiosity was so piqued. What were this town and its residents like? How did Auntie Cleo live here?

Her questions humbled her, and she sat back waiting for the few minutes she supposed it would take to get from the perimeter of Horizon to her aunt's house. She was twenty-one years old, for goodness' sake, couldn't she have visited her aunt on her own before now?

Shame heated her neck, made her shift uncomfortably on the carriage seat. Despite its padding, she'd become fidgety on the trip, her legs and bottom numb to sensation. Phee could have easily written and asked to come see her. But she had been too mired in the decision-making process of what to do with her life when she left Rose-mount. Would working as a bookkeeper in the distillery make her enough to pay for separate lodgings? Earnings from her paper-making classes would not be sufficient and she would have to teach other classes, leaving little time for her own personal pursuits. New Charleston was al-ready full to the back teeth with party planners, so the only other skill she had confidence in would be a drop in the ocean. Besides, it would take much too long to establish herself in such a cutthroat occupation. Even with her pages of lists and contingency plans, Phee had never managed to *do* anything of any import. And that indecision had prevented her progress.

But there was nothing to do about that now. Nothing except attempt to compensate for her lack of backbone by committing to laying Auntie Cleo to rest in the manner she deserved: by loving family. Phee shifted again, her travel-stiffened joints protesting loudly. While it was the least she could do, she would do it to the best of her ability.

"Here we are, miss."

Abbot's ringing voice startled Phee, and her heart fluttered with nerves she hadn't felt since departing New Charleston. She clutched one of the waxed-paper food wrappings so tightly in her fist that it crumbled and began to melt, leaving a tacky film on her palm. She hurried to gather up her things: the waxed paper went back in the sweetgrass basket. The homegoing program for her grandmother she carefully placed in her book, *The Handbook of Sighs: Poetry for the Forgotten*. This trepidation was different from her earlier worries.

The sweetness of the peanut candy was long gone, and Phee swallowed against the bile of fear that rose up in her throat. The treatment her brethren and sistren had faced under enslavement rocked her, but never before had the question of her own freedom reared its head. Jail would destroy her; she was aware of herself enough to understand that. Her hands shook and her water pressed painfully against her bladder. Success in this endeavor was her only option.

"Calm yourself," she whispered. "All will be fine and well."

The carriage pulled to a stop and Abbot spoke in his singsong manner to the horses as he secured their reins. After what felt like another small eternity, the door to the carriage opened and Abbot handed her out.

Aunt Cleo's house stood two stories tall, its bricks hand-fashioned from local oystershell and rice-ash, its sash windows curtained off to the curious. The front yard was green and neat with three steps up to a small porch where a pair of ironwork rockers sat next to each other. The house towered above her in a way that made her feel tiny, inadequate to fill its space. Even so, it gave off a lulling quality, dangling a lure to lead Phee inside.

As though called, Phee strode up those three steps to the front porch, laid her hand carefully against the brick. She gasped to find it warm, the coarseness of it reminding her of beach sand. To the right of her fingertips, she noticed a black mailbox affixed to the wall. Inside, she found an envelope with her name inscribed on it in a rounded, looping hand. Inside that lay a set of letter-wrapped keys.

"Everything all right, miss?"

Behind her, Abbot climbed the steps, one of her bags in each hand.

"Oh, yes. Thank you."

"Then I'll leave these here, if that's fine with you."

Phee glanced up from the keys in her palm. "You don't want to stay for a tea or have coffee after the drive?" She hadn't planned on being alone quite this soon.

"No, I thank you, miss. If I want to make home by full dark, I need to head on."

His gaze was earnest on hers. Phee had seen her mother refuse requests from drivers and deliverers before, and at the time, she'd attempted to scold her for her thoughtlessness. They had families and other obligations as well as her mother did. How would that be to demand he stay because she was afraid to be alone until she was settled?

"Yes, of course, Abbot. You must be ready to get back to your family." She tucked the letter away in her lunch hamper to read later. "Just let me test the key and you can be on your way."

Phee inserted the brass key into the lock and it turned with a heavy thunk. She smiled at him and fished a coin from her jacket pocket. "Well, there we are. Thank you, Abbot. For your driving and your pleasant company."

He closed his fist around the golden Stella coin and tipped his hat to her. "Thank you, miss. Be well." He looked up to the house. "And be safe."

Before she could ask what he meant, he was trundling down the steps and unhitching the horses, who had been grazing on a thick patch of grass at the edge of the property. In another blink, he was seated and clucking to the pair, who reluctantly obeyed and pulled away into a canter.

"Well." Phee's voice sounded lost in the expanse of the dying day. She gazed around her at the empty street, the tidy homes with their windows and doors shut to the encroaching evening. "Needs must."

She pushed the door to Aunt Cleo's house open and went inside.

The front door opened into a large reception room at the foot of a dark wood staircase. The interior of the house was dim and cool, and a faint scent of the sea lingered. For itself, the room was open and high-ceilinged, with a host of sofas, settees, and chairs in various rich yet worn velvet and damask fabrics. Curtains in similar fabric hung at each of the windows, drawn to give privacy. Even with its size and the curious multitude of seating, the room managed to provide a welcoming aura.

Tears prickled behind Phee's lids. It felt like exactly the kind of place Aunt Cleo would live. It felt like *her*: earnest, inviting, soft. As opposed to Rosemount's expensive and firm furnishings, this room called to her of comfort. The hardwood floors were polished and clean but not glossy enough to slip on.

After setting down her bags and jacket, Phee walked deeper into the reception room. As she went, she turned on lamps in anticipation of the coming darkness. Instead of cutting through the gathering gloom, the lamps glowed with a tender illumination that called shadows closer. They stretched along the walls, arching high and long above, around her. Unnerved, Phee rushed to find more lighting.

Along the far wall was a dial. Phee turned it, and the room brightened from the vine-shaped chandelier that clung to and crawled along the ceiling. Noontime brightness filled the room. Somehow, that much artificial light felt wrong here, and she turned the illumination down to a manageable radiance.

As she did, Phee noticed a painting on the same wall as the ceiling dimmer. It was encased in a carved and burnished frame that almost disappeared into the edges of the painting itself. Against a blue-and-white cloud-swirled sky, the main image was of two fields: one golden, the other vibrant with green. A deep divide of wet-looking black dirt separated the pair. Peering closer, Phee saw a symbol scratched into the paint on the bottom right-hand corner where the name of the artist would ordinarily be scrawled: a small letter *T*. So skillful was this painter that she reached out and touched the canvas to see if the soil was damp as it looked.

Her fingers battered up against a barrier. Funny, she'd thought the painting was only laid in the frame, not encased in glass. As she gently tapped again, expecting to feel the ridges of raised paint, all she felt was the smooth cool of glass, without seeing any. So odd. A shiver ran through her like someone had walked over her grave. Phee rubbed her hands up and down her arms to smooth away the gooseflesh. Evening was approaching and the warmth of the day fading.

Unable to resist the lure of exploring, Phee continued upstairs. She held the banister as she ascended to the second floor, the deep grain of the wood grounding her as she counted the fourteen steps. At the top, the hallway narrowed slightly from the staircase and Phee saw four doors: two on the left side of the hall, and two on the right, all offset so none of them would peer directly into the other. A window yawned at the end of the hall, covered by white sheer panels and a set of heavier pinch-pleat drapes in a teal hue, both drawn closed. She drew them open to peer out at the near-empty street.

In all her eagerness to arrive here, in all her acceptance of this being a venture she would have sole responsibility for, already the silence disturbed. It was a rough cloth dragged along her most sensitive flesh, scraping in a way that almost felt good, but left her feeling exposed, cloaked in new, not-quite-ready skin that would give at the next slightest provocation.

A search of the place would get her mind off the quiet. Busy hands, busy mind, content heart. Somewhere, she'd read those words. They'd meant nothing to her then, but at this moment they were beacons of light in darkness. She headed back to the top of the stairs and faced forward.

SIX

The first door on the left was the only one that stood open and radiating warmth; the others were closed. A double bed, neatly made, snuggled its headboard up to one wall, facing a chest of drawers made from the same carved dark wood. Each wall was painted a soft dove's-wing gray, and a few more paintings, smaller than the one downstairs, graced them. Phee's heels clicked twice on the hardwood floor before reaching a thick throw rug in a teal green that felt only slightly like she was walking through water. A curved-blade rocking chair with a cane back and padded seat nestled against the window. It shared easy access to the bedside table that was littered with books and a well-used candle.

This was certainly her aunt's bedroom. Her perfume hadn't changed in all these years: mimosa petals dusted over sugared almonds—a fragrance Phee remembered as a sweet refuge when she climbed into her aunt's lap as a small girl. Slowly, she walked around the room, fingertips gliding over the smooth armrest of the rocker, the slightly roughened texture of the canvas-bound books, and the crisp sheerness of the curtains at the window. From the rocker, she lifted a crocheted garment, fine hookwork evident in its delicacy. She shook it out to its full length, then draped the shawl over her shoulders. Almost gossamer in its lightness, the yarn was shot through with metallic color that brightened the gray to silver. The warmth such a fragile fabric provided surprised her. On the dresser sat an earring tree fashioned in delicate porcelain, a duplicate of her mother's. Had Aunt Cleo stolen this, too? When she turned it over, the inscription on the bottom told a different story:

CAS
Cleonine Atalanta Simons

Phee pressed her lips together. This entire process was going to feel like a burden if she couldn't get past the moniker of thief her mother and father still held regarding Auntie Cleo. Phee shook her head. Did anyone ever think maybe the woman solely wanted a small memento of her mother to cling to—knowing her own sister would do her best to keep it from her? As Pop had said: grief did strange things to people.

Everyone deserved grace, didn't they? At least once . . . a second chance to do the right thing. But her aunt would never have that now, would she? Tears welled in her throat and Phee swallowed them back. Her fingers curled deeply into the shawl, slipping through the holes in the needlework. She should have come to visit before now. She should have stuck up for her aunt earlier. Despite Phee's nice-nasty responses in recent years, Mama still held sway over her. She gave an unladylike snort. Oh, why hadn't she demanded to see her aunt? Or when Phee had turned eighteen, why hadn't she told Mama she was going to visit, hired a carriage with her own money, and left?

Fear.

All good daughters were raised on fear. Fear of being alone, of being talked about, of not being chosen as a lifemate. Of bearing the shame of being unwanted. So it was of utmost importance to teach your daughters to take care of others, not to learn the desires of their own hearts and the best way to fulfill them. It was easier in the long run, Phee supposed, to raise up a child who obeyed solely because they were told it was the right thing to do. Answering questions took time and patience, things her mother did not have in abundance. Fearing the wrath of a parent kept many a child in the grip of family. The idea of doing without the safety of family was a frightening prospect, especially when she knew how long her mother could hold on to an offense.

Was that any way to live?

She drifted into imaginings again, yet these were not the grand visions she usually spun for herself. Instead of castles and companies and other grand designs, Phee now imagined herself wedding Desmond, rain falling while the sun shone on their nuptials. Once married, there would be no possible escape from his grasping hands and serpentine smile. No amount of rapping with her fan would deter him from what he wanted, and it would be her duty as his wife to provide it. If she ever wanted her own wishes to take precedence, this homegoing had to be handled without her putting a foot wrong.

Phee had no answer. There was only the knowledge lapping at the shores of her mind that she had stayed in Rosemount long after it was required of her. And there was no true reason she hadn't visited her aunt besides the fact that she hadn't heard of it. On the off chance Aunt Cleo ran across her mind, she would send a letter. While she enjoyed hearing back, there was never an invitation to visit, and Phee had never asked. She had stayed wrapped up in her day-to-day life of doing Pop's accounts and attending the events her mother committed her to, all while dreaming of her own freedoms. Belatedly, she realized her mother held sway because Phee herself allowed it, not because of any real power to prevent her from following her own path.

Phee shifted, brushing her foot against something under the dresser. She fished at it with the toe of her boot, then pulled it from its hiding place. It was a pair of her aunt's shoes, soft velvet slippers the color of rich, dark wine. Phee unhooked her boots with one hand and toed them off. The slippers were cloudlike inside, and she sighed at the indulgence of them. They were beautifully cushioned, but too narrow, and they already pinched her toes. Ignoring the slight pain—it was nothing she hadn't endured at one of her cotillions—she moved to the full-length mirror and stared at her reflection.

A haze formed in the edges of her vision, blurring the

frame of the mirror until it disappeared from view. Also faded was the reflection of the room itself. What was that in the background of the mirror? Gone was the embroidered bedspread and the heavy mahogany furniture. Instead, Phee saw an orchard. A garden, possibly where she could see herself walking through the magnolia trees, their sun-warmed branches heavy with fragrant blossoms. Only it was not herself, as she was wearing a different dress in the reflection. Her hair was different, too. While still darkest brown, her reflection wore hair straightened of its usual coil, and piled on top of her head in a thick bouffant. The reflection turned and smiled at someone Phee could not see. The shawl around her reflection's shoulders glittered in the sunlight, almost as bright as the smile. A smile of pure delight that Phee could not recall seeing on herself in some time.

A fear she'd never expected gripped her. The fear she would never feel that pure unadulterated happiness she saw in the woman's face in the mirror—whether the face was hers or someone else's—and Phee trembled. Unable to resist, she reached to touch the image in front of her. Was it to see if such joy was real—to understand how someone could revel in it so?

Take it—

The voice whispered close enough in her ear for the fine hairs on the back of her neck to spark to attention. A crawling sensation skittered over her skin as the voice came again.

Take it for yourself.

Gasping, Phee threw herself bodily away from the reflection in the mirror. She stumbled backward, the backs of her knees hitting the edge of the mattress, forcing her to sit down hard. Her breath rushed out of her in a huff and she clutched the fingers of one hand to her throat, closing the shawl around the exposed skin.

She searched the mirror, but the joyous woman—whoever she had been—was gone. In its place was her own reflection: eyes wide and full of worry, edged with uncertainty. Phee calmed her breath, glanced around the room, but whatever spell the haze of the mirror had spun was now gone.

Surely, this was all her mind playing tricks. Her own consciousness speaking to her in riddles. Her own insecurities arising to tease and torment in the pinpoint perfect way only they knew. This was the first time she'd ever been on her own away from home, alone in a strange house made of materials she'd never seen, filled with a myriad of fascinating pieces of a life she wanted to be a part of. And Phee knew her mind was prone to wander toward the fanciful. Mama had warned her about reading so many books and letting her imagination wander to a world beyond the living. Conjuring was acceptable, revered even in some circles, but those who dreamed about the hereafter would be readily shunned as tetched in the head. It would make her too much like her aunt, full of strange and unnecessary notions, too curious about what came after the end.

What was wrong with being like her aunt? An accomplished woman despite it all, from what she could tell after this brief time in her home. Phee tightened her fist. Her mother . . . why must she insist on being so right all of the time? Pain flared in her hand. She hadn't realized she was still holding the earring tree, and its porcelain branches bit deeply into her palm. Sighing, she stood, and replaced it on the dresser. She needed to be made of stern stuff if she was going to get through this homegoing.

She left her aunt's bedroom, leaving behind the revealing doubts it had caused, heading for the hallway and the lure of the other closed doors. Phee tried each one in turn. The one catty-corner to her aunt's room opened without a sound when she turned the knob and peered in—the bathroom. The next door up on the same side of the hall was locked. The final door she presumed was also locked in some way; there was no visible manner of accessing it. No doorknob, no keyhole, no hinges. How odd. Never had she seen such a thing. Perhaps it was ornamental and wouldn't open at all.

Why would her aunt have an inaccessible room in her home? *Strange and unnecessary notions.* What could even be behind such a door? Maybe her aunt had been a spy during the war and this room was proof of it. Surely there had to be a way to enter in. The keys that accompanied the letter were downstairs in the hamper where she'd hurriedly dropped them; she'd retrieve them later and continue her explorations. Obviously, there was some way to enter the final room that she'd overlooked.

Daylight was fading, and shadows grew within the house, sliding sinuously along the hand-pressed brick walls that still held the fingerprints of their makers. With a click, Phee turned on the hallway light switch, and an amber illumination flickered on overhead. A gentle hum accompanied it and Phee stood directly under the frosted-glass dome encasing the lightbulbs flush-mounted to the ceiling. Somehow it made her feel secure, surrounded by all the alluring possessions of the woman she called family. A wonder crept closer to her mind: Did she ever truly know her aunt?

Perhaps she'd better fortify herself before searching any more of Aunt Cleo's house. Phee headed toward the coiling stairs still wearing her aunt's shoes. On the landing, she hastily kicked them off, peeled away her stockings, and continued to the ground floor barefoot.

Beyond the front room lay the kitchen. Here was where her aunt had spent a great deal of her time—she could tell. A sturdy table stood in the middle of the room, perfectly placed to gaze out on the backyard garden. Short stacks of books, a selection of bottles and jugs, and an array of candles formed a semicircle around the rectangular edge of what must have been a well-loved working space. Phee lit the cast iron stove and set the kettle on it. After a bustle around, she located a teapot, cup, and saucer with a subtle wave pattern. Still tired of staying seated after her journey, Phee leaned against the counter to wait for the water to boil. Absently, she lifted a brown glass jug from the table, removed the stopper. A fragrance of honey wine emerged, although the bottle itself was empty. It looked old, the handwritten label faded and peeling away at the corners, and she wondered if her father would have been able to identify it by the scent. Before the distillery had become so profitable, he'd made spirits out of honey rather than the more expensive and laborious ribbon and sugar cane syrups.

Abbot had said some matters took weeks to plan and execute if the party's family were not all in agreement on the details. He'd shaken his great head at the thought. *The dead don't wanna stay on this side longer than necessary, miss. Ain't right to keep 'em too long.* She knew well how dissention in the family affected the homegoing process, but that would be of no matter in this instance. She was the sole decider. Surely Aunt Cleo would understand if she approached this planning event with some haste.

The kettle screeched, startling her.

"Mercy!"

In the quiet of the house, her voice sounded loud, cutting through the stillness. Heart thudding, she replaced the mystery bottle on the table and slid the wailing kettle off the heat. Slowly, that stillness re-formed around her, cocooning the house once again. It seemed pleased with her; a hum she felt rather than heard ran through the floors. Her heart eased. From her lunch hamper, she pulled a bouquet of dried asters, stems wrapped in satin ribbon, then crumbled some of its petals and leaves into the teapot and poured a measure of hot water over. While she waited for her tea to steep, she drew the envelope she'd retrieved from the mailbox upon her arrival out as well. Phee jangled the keys in one hand while she read the enclosed letter.

Dear Miss St. Margaret,

    *Welcome to Horizon. My deepest sympathies to you on
the loss of your aunt. Cleonine was an honored leader in this
community and a treasured friend to me. Her absence is felt
deeply here. Despite this, it makes my heart glad to know
she will have you to give her the homegoing she wanted and
deserved.*

    *The funerary directors are eager to meet with you, and while
they understand you may wish some time to recover from your
travels, they have stressed the importance of not delaying too
long in beginning the process.*

    *If you need anything at all during your stay, please do not
hesitate to reach out to me.*

    Again, my sympathies are—

Yours,
Azalea Brown,
Horizon Council Head

SEVEN

A clattering of chimes rang out, startling Phee from the daze she had drifted into while reading the letter. It was likely only a cloak of fatigue settling upon her person after the journey, weighting her limbs and muddling her head. Whorls of floral-scented vapor rose from the teapot, the scent promising relaxation and a calming of her nervous stomach. The anticipation of it melted her bones and she slumped against the counter. The trip had taken more out of her than she'd thought. Maybe she should have had coffee instead.

Fatigue did strange things to a person. That was surely the reason for her rather strange experience upstairs. Had it been a dream or had she been visited by a spirit? There was no possibility she had fallen asleep standing in front of a mirror, but her head felt foggy, cottony, like it needed the wool shaken out of her thoughts. She must have dozed, then, if she felt this groggy. But . . . it had felt like more memory than dream. Even now, sensory notes lingered: the softness of the tender magnolia petals under her fingertips and their sugar floral fragrance clinging to her skin. Or was it the fragrance of her aunt's perfume that clung to the shawl itself? Yes, that must be it.

Again the chimes rang out, and Phee realized it was the doorbell. Who could be calling for her? Most likely it was someone offering their condolences or even someone who didn't know Aunt Cleo had passed on. She would have to inform them of the news of her passing. Phee patted her hair, checking for loose coils, then strode to the front of the house, letter in hand. After a deep breath, she donned the smile she reserved for company and pulled the door wide. That same smile remained frozen in place as she came face-to-face with the stranger on the doorstep.

A middle-aged woman, thin as laces, stood on the porch with a large kitchen towel–covered basket in her hands. At her feet stood two large bags made of crocus, the rough brown fabric stretched with its mysterious contents. When she saw Phee, her round, liquid-brown eyes widened.

"Cleo?" she said, confusion in her voice.

"Oh, no. I'm her niece, Phaedra, here to handle the homegoing. Please call me Phee." She reached out to take the basket from the woman's arms, wondering how such a small lady could carry all of those packages at once.

"Oh . . . yes. Of course."

Phee couldn't help but note what sounded like a hint of disappointment in her visitor's voice, and she clutched the basket closer to her chest. Gorgeous smells emanated from within: buttery, rich, and warm. Phee's stomach grumbled so loud she almost missed the woman's self-introduction.

"I'm Azalea Brown. Zaye. I live at the top of the main

road up there." She indicated with a toss of her head. "The white stonework place."

"Oh yes?"

"Looks like you got my letter and the keys." Her smile was dimpled in both cheeks, and her ebony hair was oiled and smoothed back from a middle part into two coiling braids. If she'd heard Phee's stomach protesting, she was too polite to mention it.

"Oh!" Phee looked down at the slightly crumpled letter peeking out from where her fingers curled around the basket. "I did, thank you."

"Brought you some provisions, too."

Phee's face heated. What was wrong with her—leaving this woman to stand on the front steps? "My manners must have left me along the road. My apologies. Please come in for a cup of tea." She shifted the weight of the basket to one hand and reached out with the other. "Let me get those bags for you."

The older woman waved away her offer of help. "That's all right about my burdens; I'm used to it. But tea sounds nice."

Zaye hefted the two bags with so little effort, Phee blinked. She followed Phee inside to the kitchen, but from the familiarity with which the older woman set the bags onto the countertops Phee suspected she had been here many times before.

While Phee fussed around looking for plates and putting the kettle back on the stove, her visitor confirmed her suspicions. Zaye unpacked fresh fruit, ribbon cane stalks, a bag each of ground coffee and loose tea. There were also trays of cooked food, both savory and sweet: stew crab, red pea rice, spicy green beans with baby turnips, boiled green peanuts, and a crispy-top sweet potato pone with dark, crusty corners of crystallizing brown sugar and butter. She couldn't resist sampling, and sighed at the flavor melting over her tongue.

Phee grinned when she heard Zaye's chuckle.

"I'll tell Mrs. Brenda you like her pone."

"Please tell her I love it. Mama won't make it because it's too much work. Too hard on the hands."

Zaye tilted her head to consider Phee. "It's the shawl."

"I'm sorry?"

"That made you look to me like Cleo for a while. She wore it often." Zaye drew a serving tray from a cupboard and laid it on the table.

Phee smoothed her hands over the fabric. It had seemed so much more vibrant earlier when she'd put it on. Now it looked like any other secondhand garment: good quality, good condition, a little faded by time. "Oh yes. I found it in Auntie's room and I . . . well, I liked it."

"Looks right on you, too."

"Thank you."

"Coffee or tea?" The kettle whistled and Zaye lifted it with a dishcloth. "I am sorry. So used to making myself at home here."

Phee assured her there was no offense as she placed several tiny honey cakes and stone-fruit tarts on a palm leaf–shaped plate she found in the china cabinet for them to share, but left the bread rolls and rice bread and especially the pone for when she was alone later. The women sat in the dining room. It was large enough to seat eight, but they chose to sit across from each other on the side closest to the doors leading out to the garden.

"There aren't a lot of people in this town," Phee commented while pouring a cup of tea for her guest. Phee had watched carefully while the carriage entered the town and moved through its center to Aunt Cleo's home. The streets were not only quiet, the sound of inhabitants was almost none. Animal sounds mostly: frogs, nightbirds, the drone of cicadas, and the distant sound of hooves on the blacktop road. In the growing gloom, she watched the wink of fireflies darting.

"Not at the moment," Zaye replied, adding a cube of golden-brown sugar to her cup. "But that's a good thing."

Phee raised her eyebrows and her cup to her lips. "It is?"

"For us, yes. You see"—Zaye shifted in her chair to get comfortable—"this is a shelter town. By its nature, it is a transitory place. Your aunt knew what it was to be without a place where you're welcome. Horizon is that shelter for all who are without."

Not knowing what to say to that revelation, Phee kept quiet. Luckily her guest was happy to fill the gap in her knowledge. "It's a rest stop for most, a place to stay long enough to get your bearings, get your strength back, get your head right enough to move on to where you're supposed to be." She chuckled. "Or at least where you're going next."

Phee smiled around her cup. Instead of fighting to get back into the family's good graces, her aunt had created a place for herself and welcomed others in. Then without warning, a fierce worry nipped at Phee, drawing blood. The magnitude of what Aunt Cleo had accomplished in her life without anyone to help humbled her. Would Phee be able to give her aunt the final service she deserved and avoid the threat of incarceration? Her stomach boiled, the tea turning acidic in her mouth.

"That's just like Auntie to do for others when—" She stopped, unsure if she should finish with *when no one was doing for her.* What, if anything, had Aunt Cleo shared with Horizon and its residents? It seemed Auntie and Zaye had been friends, but still . . . that didn't mean she'd revealed all of her troubled family history during the course of that friendship.

When she glanced over at her companion, Zaye smiled ruefully at her. "Were you going to say 'when no one thought to help her'?"

Phee gave a brief grimace. She added herself to that number of people who hadn't lifted a finger to check on her aunt outside of a few letters and cards.

"Something like that," she admitted to her teacup.

A pause descended in the room, buffeted by the sounds of night edging closer and the faraway call of the sea. It wasn't an uncomfortable silence between them, rather an allowance of space for the truth to fully enter and breathe.

Finally, Phee spoke. "I wanted to come visit her before now. There was never a good time." She shook her head, tea threatening to spill over the rim of the cup as her hands trembled. "That's not true. I didn't make the time."

Zaye nodded. "Life often gets in the way of what we want to do. So does death. Speaking of," she said, easing further back into the chair, "are you ready for the funeral directors? No use putting it off. They've offered to come after the dinner hour."

"Tonight?" Phee gaped. She was already tired and she hadn't done anything except sit in a carriage and peer into a few rooms. And now they expected her to conduct business?

"Yes. It isn't good for the dead to wait too long." Zaye cut off a piece of tart shell with her pastry fork, and ate it while watching Phee closely. It seemed the older woman was assessing her with a disturbingly neutral manner.

Just as Abbot said. This was not the time for the dead to wait on her to sort out her regrets and hesitations. This was the time for her to wait on the dead. She should not have told Abbot to keep a leisurely pace getting here; she should have made haste. Yet another thing about planning a homegoing that she didn't know. Deep breath. *This is what you promised to do, Phaedra. You had no idea what awaited you, but it's far too late to renege.*

"They can come tomorrow—first thing," Phee promised. "I'd like tonight to myself if that's all right."

"Of course." Zaye smiled. "I'll arrange it."

"I . . ." Phee pressed her lips together, unsure of how pointed she could be with this stranger. But Azalea Brown knew her aunt and maybe she would have some insight as to what kind of service to plan.

The admission was bitter in her mouth. "I don't know what to do for her."

Zaye patted her shoes against the floor while she ate another bite of tart. Napkin against her mouth, she swallowed. She laid the square of starched linen in her lap once again before speaking. "It's understandable you feel a bit lost. 'Overwhelmed' might be a better word."

"Both apply."

Zaye blew out a breath Phee belatedly realized was a chuckle. "I'm certain, especially as this is your first one."

"I suppose I'm lucky in not having experienced much loss."

"Lucky," Zaye repeated, her tone without inflection. Phee got the distinct feeling she'd said entirely the wrong thing, but the older woman's flat tone was gone with her next words. She fluttered a well-groomed hand in a "worry not" manner and sipped from the teacup. "Mayhap you'll have an easier time of it if you follow Cleo's instructions."

Phee leaned forward so swiftly her cup clattered back into the saucer. "There are *instructions*?"

Zaye's liquid eyes widened, showing a perimeter of white around the dark. Phee apologized for her outburst and the woman settled, albeit while keeping a watchful gaze on her host.

"Not formal instructions, no." Zaye delicately wiped her fingers, then folded the napkin in thirds and placed it on the table. "But most people here keep an envelope or something with requests for their last, telling a trusted friend or family member where to find it when the time comes."

Trusted friend.

Zaye had mentioned "friend" first, before "family member," and Phee wondered if the woman was hurt Auntie hadn't put the instructions in her care. Or why she hadn't sent her instructions directly to Rosemount, trusting someone in the family would step up to pomp for her when the time came?

Perhaps because Aunt Cleo knew her sister all too well. Knew Mama wouldn't ever pomp for her. Knew even death wouldn't be enough for her to forgive.

After a pause where Phee could hear the night crawling closer, Zaye tilted her head back a moment, then smoothed her hair with her palm. "I gather from the look on your face, you don't have such a something."

"No, I would have thought you or someone here would. We're . . . that is, we haven't been . . ." Phee sat her cold tea on the table and fussed with the empty crumb-dusted tray. ". . . especially close these past years."

When she chanced a look up, Zaye was staring out into the garden. "So I gathered. I never asked, but I gathered." She paused as if to speak, then changed her mind. After another moment of contemplation, she stood and straightened out her skirt. "I'd better be off, then. I must contact the funeral directors to tell them to arrive at eight o'clock sharp."

"Eight?" Phee's voice was full of horror at the thought of visitors so early.

Zaye smiled at her reaction. "Yes, I thought you might want to sleep in a bit."

Phee followed her guest to the door, sad to see her company leave. She wasn't keen on being alone in the house again so soon. Having good companionship and conversation were ideal, but having another body in the house with her even if they weren't speaking was of comfort.

"Thank you for the tea," Zaye said, on the threshold.

"Thank you for the food. I'm grateful." Phee was pensive, this new information of the likelihood of instructions lying somewhere within these walls adding to the duty list in her mind. *Who will do the body?*

"Of course. The grieving shouldn't have to work to feed themselves. If you need any more, just say."

Zaye halted on the porch with her back to Phee, the setting sun outlining her small, spare frame in bursts of orange fire. When she turned, the dying light behind obscured her face but her voice rang clear.

"Search this place, Phaedra. Cleo wouldn't have left here without making her wishes known." Her heels clicked on the stone steps as she tipped away from the house. "Don't forget—eight o'clock on tomorrow," she called over her shoulder.

Phee watched Zaye leave, the woman who had been a better friend to her aunt than she ever was a niece. Yet another concern lifted its head. Would Aunt Cleo have wanted her for this duty of pomp? Would she have trusted her with such an important duty when she knew Phee had little experience with such matters?

She wrapped her arms around herself to keep the chill filling her spirit at bay. If Phee found these instructions and they asked for Zaye, what would she do? Zaye had been better support to her aunt than anyone else in the family, even herself. As a close companion and the council head of Horizon, the woman must feel at least somewhat put out by Phee's presence. Not to mention, she must have some concern that Phee wouldn't be up to the task. How could she even speak over her aunt at the service when she hadn't set eyes on Auntie Cleo since that fateful afternoon? All she had were her own decade-old memories, dozens of letters, and a desire to right a wrong she had no part in committing.

As the sun slipped out of sight, Phee wondered if planning a funeral was enough to make up for the passage of years.

EIGHT

Alone again. But the house felt different this time. Almost as if it now knew Phee was looking for the secret it had been charged with hiding. As she turned away from the front door, the house felt braced for her invasion, instead of the sigh of pleasured welcome she'd felt when she first arrived.

Nonsense. The house had no more changed in the past hour of Zaye's visit than she herself had. Spotting her bags still on the floor of the reception room, Phee huffed and strode over to them. Now that she had the rest of the evening to herself, she could prepare for bed. She set her carpetbag on one of the settees and opened the top to search for her nightdress and sleep cap. As she searched through the bag, she found the agricole Pop had given her. From his reserve aged collection, no less!

She carefully removed the box and opened it; a fragrance of buffed oak warmed her from the inside. The contents of the bottle would warm her even more, but she was sure tougher times were coming and she should save the precious liquor for those moments. Still, it was heartening to have it on hand. Pop was always the more encouraging of her parents. He never raised his voice, even when he intervened with her mother on Phee's behalf. Phee smiled, gazing at the gift. He was so generous with what little time he had aside from running the distillery and campaigning to join the governing body of the Freedman's Bureau. Whenever she approached him for advice, he always gave her his counsel. She closed the box. The right time for this would come.

Phee strode to the kitchen, as that room had felt the warmest, the most like home when she'd first arrived. Not that it resembled the kitchen at home in any way, it was much too rustic, but it held the comforts of a well-appointed home. Phee took a sweet wafer from the basket Zaye had brought. Its nut-brown sheen gave way to a buttery crispness that soothed her as she washed and put away the few dishes.

Where would she start looking for an envelope of her aunt's wishes for her burial? Phee wiped down the tabletop and counter, then hung the damp cloth on the edge of the sink to dry. On one hand, her concerns about being able to correctly guess what her aunt would have wanted for her funeral were somewhat alleviated. On the other, she would have to locate these instructions—and quickly. If they even existed. Her aunt was young in death, having only just passed forty years of life, and perhaps she had not expected to pass beyond so soon. But Zaye had suggested searching, so there must be good reason to believe some notes lay waiting to be found. These were to be some of the most important decisions she would make in this final show of care, and having a guide from the decedent herself would help infinitely.

Perhaps it would have helped to know where her grandmother had kept her envelope of the instructions before her death, but it was unlikely Mama would tell her, even if she managed to get a messenger there. Surely it had been somewhere at Rosemount—her grandmother had been born and died in that house—but with twelve rooms, it was impossible to guess where it could have resided until found. Preparation for bed could wait. Best to begin looking. At least there were only seven rooms here.

Phee opened drawer after drawer in what felt like an endless space. She found serving trays, bottles of dried herbs, and even a few contraptions she had never seen before— what purpose they had she could only surmise. A forked branch, almost as long as Phee's arm. A metal, clawlike contraption with wicked blades attached to a short wooden handle? It seemed monstrous and Phee was enchanted by the idea of discovering its use. Her gaze fell on a set of pale green demijohn bottles in a cabinet and she reached for a round-bellied one. Even half full, it was heavier than she'd expected. The label that managed to cling to its side was faded, partially torn away. She tried to pull the cork out, but it didn't budge. Frustrated, she replaced it and lifted a different jar, this one wide-mouthed and lined with a sheen of condensation. She tapped on the jug lightly while peering into it. Some kind of moss grew inside, dense and green-dark. It seemed a deliberate thing—not an accident of forgetfulness that allowed this moss to thrive. A small part of the moss was missing, almost as if it had been intentionally rolled back like the open mouth of a grave. Within, the turned-back hole looked wet, raised, like the black earth separating the two fields in the painting she'd seen when she arrived. Again, a glass barrier prevented further exploration. Phee returned the jug to its place with a trembling hand.

Even after turning all of the cupboards inside out and checking for false backs and bottoms, she was still no wiser as to the location of the instructions or the uses of the instruments. Knowing Aunt Cleo better could have helped in her search. Phee thought of calling at Zaye's home, but she knew the woman was off coordinating the funeral directors' visits for tomorrow morning. She shuddered. How many would there be? Six? Eight? Pop's worried comments suggested she would be overwhelmed, and his lack of belief in her rankled. She was bright, she was capable.

She was filthy.

Her hands were covered in a layer of fine dust and grit that all old homes seemed to gather if not dusted daily. Her forearms, where she had rolled up the sleeves of her blouse, itched with grime that grayed her brown skin. A coil of her hair brushed her face, but she refused to tuck it away with her hands or wrists. As tired as she was, she had no desire to wash unruly locks tonight.

An ache emanated from the small of her back, radiating out from a knot of tension in the muscle. So much lifting and reaching and crouching and pulling—she wasn't used

to this much strain. No matter. It was temporary—a pain to distract her from rogue thoughts of how much easier this would have been if she had only come to Horizon when Aunt Cleo was alive. Proved to her aunt and to herself that she could exist outside of Rosemount. No. She shook her head. She didn't want to exist. She wanted to thrive.

She was her own person, had her own thoughts and ideas. Phee blew the irritating coil of hair out of her face, then kneeled again to open what she hoped was the last cupboard in this room. Her body cried at her to stop but she needed to keep on, push forward to drown out the little demon voices that giggled and hissed:

You are your own person far too late. Too late to help anyone but yourself.

Pomping. Doing this little ceremony, is it enough?

Wouldn't your aunt have preferred to see you here when she still lived?

Phee sat down hard on the floor, her traveling skirt trapping a huff of air that burst as she landed on the brushed stone. She would do everything in her power to give her aunt the ceremony she wanted. Even if it took her searching every cranny of this house. She looked to her left, across the rest of the kitchen to the back door.

On a sigh, she said out loud, "And garden."

She replaced the punch bowl and cups she'd removed and closed the cupboard. Getting to her feet, she made her way to the back door and twitched back the curtain to gaze at the garden. During her search night had fallen, but there was enough moonlight to see the garden hadn't been looked after in some time. Grasses overgrown, statues unrecognizable. The candles she'd lit during Zaye's visit reflected in the glass, joining the dance of the fireflies. All the many sounds of the night blended into a low hum that vibrated the dark and quickened Phee's heart. A path lay in the garden, barely visible under a blanket of weaving vines and clumping moss.

Worry placed its frosty fingers on Phee, the spiked tips of its fingernails digging in, dragging down her spirits along with her shoulders. Her back sang to her its pain. How would she do all of this? Would she need to take care of the garden as well? Sell the house? Yes, of course—all of it was wrapped up in this final act of care.

Finally, she was beginning to understand her mother's concern—her sharp clapping—as she looked out on the dense overgrowth. It was to reinforce her words, get them through Phee's thick head that she wasn't ready for this responsibility. Tomorrow, she had to be up, dressed, and ready for company by eight o'clock and her arms were leaden. If she wasn't able to make the right choices, evaluate these funeral directors on their abilities, and put together the appropriate service, her freedom could be forfeit.

No. There was no reason to dwell on fantasies. Certain realities were in front of her: she was a day's carriage ride away—albeit a leisurely journey—from her family's support, she was alone in the home of a woman she revered, yet barely knew. There were instructions somewhere in this house that must be found and visitors arriving directly after breakfast. The strangeness of the house with its sealed rooms and vision-giving mirrors, and grave-yards in jars, was only one more item to contend with on her own.

Or was she on her own in this house? The memory of that otherworldly voice whispering in her ear made her question her solitude. She had heard it so clearly, felt it against her skin. The need to follow its suggestions fright-ened her. At the same time, the thought of an adventure beyond her dreams thrilled her mightily. Phee rubbed her neck to rid herself of the crawling sensation from earlier. If she wanted to succeed, she must keep to her task. There would be time for fancy later. She pushed away from the door, blew out the candle, trudged upstairs for a bath, then bed.

It was far, far too late to do anything else.

By the time Phee reached the landing, the heavy twill fabric of her skirt dragged at her, slowing her pace to a shuffle. Each footstep up the stairs brought more weariness. A long soak in the bath would restore her. But which room had the bath? It wasn't en suite like her parents' and she wished she'd wandered through the entire house before now.

But she had already done that, hadn't she? Why couldn't she remember? She could recall her aunt's bedroom with distinct clarity, but the rest of the upstairs felt like she'd never encountered it before. Were the curtains always teal blue? Had they been open or closed? Her head was all a mix-up and she was desperate to rest. However, there were only three remaining rooms on this floor, so she pushed herself forward.

Beyond her aunt's room, the door was locked. Surprised, she turned the handle again, hoping it was only jammed. But no avail. The keys that had arrived in the letter from Zaye were on the kitchen table—she remembered that much—and the thought of traipsing down there and back up was more than she could bear.

Later, she promised herself.

Across the hall from the locked room, the door had no doorknob, no handle, no keyhole.

A memory flittered about the edge of her senses, but for the life of her, she could not grasp it. This door was here earlier, wasn't it? Phee stepped back a pace to peruse the door again. Varnished oak like all the others, it seemed normal save for the inability to open it. Aunt Cleo was no puzzle player or game-smith, so there wouldn't be a trick to accessing the room. Or would there? Phee pressed her palms against the door, hoping the right pressure in the right place would reveal its secrets. She kneeled, inspecting the entire doorjamb to deduce where the hinges were. Finding nothing, she stood and backed away. If someone took this great a care to seal something away, maybe it should not be revealed. Anything could be behind that door, and whatever it was, Phee was here with it.

"I'm not thinking clearly," she said. The sound of her voice was at first stark, then it faded away slowly like ripples on a pond. She imagined the walls consuming her words, desperately hungry for any sound. "First thing in the morning, I'll figure it out."

The final door revealed her desired destination. The bathroom held a large copper tub against the far wall, its smooth, gleaming inside a distinct difference from the roughened verdigris patina that clung to metals submerged in ocean waters for eons. A gray concrete vanity sink and black commode took up the left wall. Unusual pieces that didn't perfectly match, but somehow went together. From under the sink, she took a towel, washrag, and a cake of soap and sat them on the commode lid, then turned on the tap. She unbuttoned her dark purple skirt and unlaced the mustard-yellow petticoat beneath, the combination landing in a heap like a deflated hot-air balloon collapsing to earth. Her blouse followed, leaving Phee in her chemise and drawers. She touched her hair to check that it was secured up and out of the water's way. It was loud in the room; the wash of water sounding industrial, the way the waves of spirits sloshed against the gigantic copper kettles in Pop's distillery.

Steam came up off the troubled surface of the water. Phee lost herself in watching it rise. She rocked back and forth on her bare feet, arms wrapped around herself in spite of the growing warmth of the room. She felt guided to enter the water, to sink beneath it. Not to end things, but to begin them. The desire to listen to the water from within grew in her mind until she could not ignore it.

Hear me.

Heed the water.

Phee shucked herself free of her chemise and drawers; her hands moved of their own free will. No, someone else's hands guided her own. The scent of the water called, briny and blood-warm. Light reflected off the copper, lending a bronze hue to the surrounding tiled wall.

Submerge yourself.

Heed.

It burned.

Phee yelped, drew her foot back from the tub. How had she even thought to try to step into it? She held her hand under the rush of the tap, only to find it ran cold. She turned it off with a wrench of her hand. How was the water steaming only a moment ago? Her foot stung, the skin on it scalded soft and pulsing. She laid the towel down on the floor as a rug and retrieved another out of the vanity sink's cabinet.

"What is happening?" she whispered to herself as she stirred the water with the washrag until hot and cold united. Having plumbing indoors was a newfangled invention; perhaps this occurred from time to time out here in a place as remote as Horizon. It had never occurred at Rosemount that she knew of. "Sleep, I need sleep."

She'd gotten precious little rest last night, the anticipation of the journey keeping her staring at the ceiling, her thoughts churning, churning with *what if*s and *well, then*s. Much of her confidence stemmed from her mother's protests, a pushing against the succor of family, a scrambling toward the unknown with the surety of ignorance and childlike naivety.

This time when she stepped gingerly in the bath, the water's embrace was kind. Deeper than the one at home, the lip of this bathtub reached her shoulder when she was seated and the water level covered her breasts. She reclined, slipping deeper in, the copper itself now warmed through. Phee soaped the rag and washed herself with as much speed as she could muster, the warm bath sapping the rest of her remaining energy.

She braced her hands on the lip of the tub and stood, water running off her skin in rivulets. Carefully, she lifted one leg high to clear the edge of the tub. One damp hand slid out from under her. Phee gasped, scrambling to catch herself before her face hit the rolled metal. Instead, her knee hit the roughened verdigris exterior and it grated against her bare, bath-tender skin. She cursed at the sharp knock of pain when she landed on the floor tiles. She blinked and her lashes brushed against the warm metal.

"Magician's mercy," she whispered.

She drew herself up from where she kneeled on the floor and reached into the water, intending to squeeze dry the cloth and use it to shore up her grip. Movement underneath the water rippled the surface and Phee shrieked, falling back. In the soapy water, she'd seen a reflection staring back. Her, but not. Something odd in the eyes. Something unknowable. Naked, she let her entire body sink under its gaze. The cool floor brought her out of her stupor quickly, seeping into her bath-warmed skin. She got to her knees slowly, then her feet, careful of the slick surface under her. With the aid of one hand against the brick, and the other clutching a towel around her nudity, Phee made her way to the bedroom.

This was nothing, she told herself while she applied some of her aunt's skin cream to her body, an amber-scented balm, and slipped into her nightdress. Her head reeled with the potent fragrance of the cream. It clung to her skin, heating it against the night's chill. *Nothing at all.* She placed fresh sheets on the bed and climbed beneath the covers, sighing at the luxury of laying her bones down.

Everything is fine. It is all fine. Nothing a good night of sleep wouldn't correct by morning.

NINE

The funeral directors came in droves.

Fidgeting on Auntie Cleo's wingback chairs, edging away from each other on the lion claw–footed sofa so as to not crush the fine linen of their fine suits or catch their glittering bracelets on the fading brocade fabric, the funeral directors tried to outdo each other.

Some jawed as they waited, speaking large about their company's superiority and how the others should save their time and go home now. Of course the founder of the town would want the best send-off, and their service was it. Most of them, however, waited furtively, the impatience in their eyes twining with an eagerness to get the agreements and contracts signed. They shifted their weight, widened their shoulders, doing all they could to take up the most space.

Phee had one of Zaye's biscuits drizzled with sun-warmed, salted honey along with her tea as she watched the flood of funeral directors invade the sitting room, and knew it would be the last she ate for a long while. It had been a struggle to force herself up and out of bed at the sound of mourning doves in the tree outside the window cooing the sunrise. She'd slept heavily, but not restfully. Her sleep had been thick with clinging dreams of water, or perhaps something more viscous and difficult to swim through. She felt drained, her limbs only tacked onto her body.

After washing her hands in the kitchen and rubbing a bit of oil into them, she entered the sitting room. Zaye had been kind enough to provide a schedule of appointments, but apparently that had no bearing on the proceedings. They all arrived at the same time, frightfully eager, dreadfully spry.

Every one of them was coffin sharp, decked out in tailored suits to fit the multitude of their sizes, shapes, and frames. Creases starched, hair freshly cut and dressed. Phee felt underdressed in her white cotton blouse and midnight-blue broadcloth skirt, but she knew this was part of the process. She was the one they had to impress. Best to go ahead and get on.

"Mr. Facey?" Phee called from her list.

A middle-aged man in an oxblood-and-cream seersucker suit and matching suede spectators stood. One hand grasped his lapel and the other held a hat that was . . . unfortunate-looking in its design and color.

"I'm the one and only, young miss. First choice, best choice."

Phee's lips bent into a polite smile. "Please, come in. I'm Phaedra St. Margaret."

Mr. Facey turned and whispered something to the man on the settee who had taken his vacated space, and the man scoffed, then shooed him away with a ring-laden hand. She ushered peacocking Mr. Facey into her aunt's office, a smallish room nestled between the kitchen and the sitting room. Inside was a simple writing desk and two chairs that took up much of the space.

Thankfully, she and her aunt must have been of a similar height, as the kneehole under the desk fit her legs well. Phee cracked open a window to let out the fragrance of boiled linseed polish that hovered in the room, and sat, inviting Mr. Facey to do the same. Phee ran her fingers over the edge of desk, following the crimped pie-crust design and enjoying the brilliance of the gleaming surface. A porcelain desk set made up of a letter rack, pen-and-ink holder, and fountain pen added to the elegant yet businesslike style of the room. She looked up to find him still standing, looking down on her with an air of concern that was slow to clear.

"Sympathies to you, young miss," he began in a salesman's patter. "I'm sure you're not in the frame of mind to want to worry yourself about the final preparations for your auntie. Great woman, she was. Great, great."

"Oh, did you know her personally?" Phee asked.

He clutched his bird-of-paradise hat to his chest. "Not me myself, but you know. A body does hear great things about great people."

"Yes, of course." Phee again motioned to the chair across from her aunt's desk to hide her disappointment. Would this entire experience be people who didn't know her aunt advising on what was best? "Please sit."

"I'll stand, if you don't mind, young miss. Better for my presentation, you see."

Young miss. The moniker grated, especially in the tone this man used. As if he were reminding her of her place and his superior knowledge. His knowledge might surpass hers, but she was due her own courtesies. "Please call me Miss St. Margaret. Or Miss Phaedra, if you prefer."

The man blinked as if no one had ever corrected him before. "Sure, sure."

He tumbled over his next words, thrown off course by her polite correction. To cover his fluster, he drew a folded pamphlet from the pocket of his jacket and put it on the desk in front of her. After, he cleared his throat and launched into a speech that would rival any sermon she'd ever heard in duration and in doomsday language.

It was everything in her to endure his rehearsed words, his flamboyant arm-waving, and that hat, which he had perched on top of his head to great—if not positive—effect.

"We will put your aunt to rest in a manner never seen anywhere. Our best service is the top one on that list. Open the booklet there." Without waiting for her to do so, he rushed over to the desk and pulled the paper from her hand and spread it on the desk. He jabbed at the ornate writing. "You see it there. You wouldn't have to lift a finger. We'll take care of it all. Planning, dressing, food, burial, and the service! Whew . . . Like no one else."

He leaned forward, much too close, and Phee was grateful for the broadness of her aunt's desk separating them.

"She would have to have the best, you see that, don't

you, Miss Margaret? A great woman deserves that. Don't skimp. Don't do that to your auntie, will you?"

"I'll be sure not to," Phee responded crisply, taking the fountain pen in hand so she wasn't tempted to wring Mr. Facey's neck. This was not what she'd expected at all. He couldn't even call her by the correct name. She didn't bother to correct him this time, as she would not be using his services for anything. She stood and walked to the door, back stiff. "Thank you, Mr. Facey. I appreciate your time and, er . . . presentation."

Facey followed, yanking off the hat. "Remember, first is best." He did not glance at the waiting directors as he took his leave.

She absently tapped the pen's fine metal nib with her fingertip while watching him, the front door yawning open to encourage his exit. That was a farce suited only as a skit for children. Surely this was not the best Horizon had to offer. She turned from the departing Facey to find a host of similarly eager faces watching her. At that moment, she realized she'd left the schedule in the office. No matter. Suppressing a shudder, she called, "Who is next, please?"

A pleasantly round-faced man stood and made his path to her in a pigeon-toed strut. "Mr. Spring, Miss St. Margaret. How do you do?"

"I'm well, thank you." Already more comfortable with this man's demeanor after the ill-fated Mr. Facey, she ushered him inside and sat behind the desk.

"So sorry to hear about your aunt's passing. I didn't know her well, but she certainly will be missed in Horizon."

Phee thanked him as she replaced the pen in its holder. "Do you live in Horizon, Mr. Spring?"

"No, no." He shook his round, brown head. "A few towns away, in Raglo, but my business takes me all over— Horizon, Alkalu, even New Charleston."

"Ah, that is where I live."

An odd light flashed in the older man's eyes. Phee didn't catch the meaning of the glint, but decided it was recognition of a shared communion. "Is that right? I handle business there quite frequently."

"Oh, that is good. My mother only uses Manning's for our family's homegoings, but I inquired there and they do not handle services outside of the city."

"No need. Plenty of business in the city itself." His round face bobbed, reminding Phee of an inflated balloon on a windy day. "Do you have her exact written wishes for her last? We would, of course, follow them to the letter."

His asking for the documents put Phee in the mind that Mr. Spring was far more the professional than the overbearing Mr. Facey. She began to relax, thinking this decision all but made.

"Not as of yet," she admitted. "But Ms. Azalea has assured me the documents are here in this house."

Before her eyes, Mr. Spring's face shifted from the smiling round balloon to something fearsome. The jovial look slid from his face like greasepaint, leaving the ill-concealed gaze of a predator. He seemed to enlarge, a grotesque swelling of body, a dead thing left in foul standing water. The change was so swift it took Phee's breath. She pressed herself back in her chair, the hard wood and stiff velvet a thin comfort.

"No papers?" His voice . . . oh, it was a frightful thing. A veneer of civility insufficient to cloak the need to grasp, pick apart, devour, and discard. "That is no concern, Miss St. Margaret. We will create the perfect package for you."

The satchel came from nowhere. In a flash it was on the desk, opened, its contents spilling out like matter from a squeezed shrimp head. His stumpy hands ran through the wash of slick papers, rummaging. He shoved testimonials from prior clients under her nose, then swept them away into a pile before she could grasp them.

"You can read these later, to your heart's content. But you should not delay your aunt's services any longer. The dead do not like to stay with the living. You don't want to get on the wrong side of the spirits, do you?"

While his tone was deferential, the set of his jaw, the twist of his lip were contemptuous. She had enough experience to know when someone's words did not match their manner.

"Of course not," he continued without her reply, placing daguerreotypes of deceased persons she did not know on the wide expanse of the desk. "It is well worth any cost to remain in good stead."

Her ire rose. "Enough, Mr. Spring."

"But these are some of my finest work. You must see . . ."

All she saw were their eyes. Open. Vacant. And the varied hues of their brown skin, covered not in the expected death pallor, but in a tight, ashy mask that looked as though she could work a fingernail under it and lift demise from their faces. While their arms were crossed over their hearts as was the custom, their hands were clenched, fingers drawn back into claws. The dead stared out at Phee from behind their masks, boring into her, asking for release from this final ignominy. Angry tears pricked her eyes. These poor people did not rest easy. She would never subject Aunt Cleo to the ministrations of this man.

"Enough!"

The volume of her voice startled them both. Phee's heart went out to whoever these people were, and to whoever thought Spring could give their loved ones proper final care. It was beyond a travesty to see, so she pushed the images toward the man with the heel of her palm. Funeral director, indeed!

Phee gathered herself, bringing every ounce of breeding from her one and twenty years with her parents to bear in order not to yowl at the man for the humiliating way he had treated these people. She balled her hand into a fist, her nails biting into her palm to steady her whirling emotion. Instead, she berated him in as controlled a tone as she could muster.

"You sent people to their last like this? How *dare* you? White powder . . . eyes open . . . The indignity of it makes me ill, Mr. Spring."

The man morphed again. His eyes before were greedy predator slits in his bobbing balloon of a face. Now they widened with shock for a long moment as he looked past her to something she could not see. Then he frowned and scraped the photographic papers into his bag.

"A woman, a young one at that," he muttered darkly.

Phee folded her arms across her chest. As she opened her mouth to protest, the fountain pen rose from its holder and flew like a dart across the desk toward Mr. Spring. He yelped and dodged, the metal nib sinking into the wooden frame on the wall behind him. Both Phee and Mr. Spring stared at the area where his shoulder had been and the pen now wobbled. Phee recovered first, pressing her fingers to her open mouth while Mr. Spring babbled an unsteady retort.

"I know you . . . your family. Your mother despairs of you finding a husband." He sneered. "I see now why."

"I don't think you *do* see, Mr. Spring. At all. Not if those photographs are any indication." Phee stood and opened the office door wide, gesturing for him to take his leave.

Spring tried to storm out of the office, but only managed to bob along like a toy in a brisk wind. The front door slammed. Phee noticed the rest of the assembled funeral directors perk up, straightening their collars, shuffling stacks of crisp paperwork. Still, they filled each seat, leaned against every large piece of furniture. An air of bounded determination leached from those assembled and swirled within the room, a choking fog that made Phee want to run for the careful quietude of Rosemont.

The only way out of this was through.

She went back into the office, pulled the pen free, and

placed it once again in its holder. Back at the door, she placed her smile firm, hoping it wasn't a rictus. "Who is next, please?"

A severely dressed woman stood at Phee's words. While Phee wore supportive underpinnings—her mother demanded it—they could not rival the ones that had created the figure before her. After taking the offered seat, the woman patted her perfectly sculpted hair and spoke.

And spoke.

And spoke.

Phee had no opportunity to wedge in a comment or observation amidst the funerary's monologue. Hymns and which hymnals, processional and recessional order, appropriate paper quality for programs, suitable attire for the deceased and the grieving.

Once the older woman's questions began, Phee's mind whirled, unable to grasp the queries themselves, much less the responses. Coffin or casket? Did the miss have a hairdresser for the deceased in mind or would she want to hire a desairologist for the purpose? Where would the location of service and the burial be? Would they be the same place? Who was attending? Oh, and of course flowers . . . What kind would your aunt prefer?

Phee rocked side to side in the chair, a habit she used to soothe herself when overwhelmed. The regular motion provided an artificial comfort, allowing her to function for a little while longer.

Kindly, she stopped the woman's rush of words. Phee wasn't sure she even recalled the woman introducing herself—Mrs. Renderr, maybe?—and thanked her for her thoroughness. She would have to contact her later once she was able to consult her aunt's wishes in more depth. The woman left a sheaf of paper, at least two options addressing each question she'd asked, then left with a nod and the press of cool, firm fingers on the back of Phee's hand.

Phee called for the next. She nodded absently as the queue of funeral directors filed into her aunt's office one by one to give their planned presentations. Her ears rang with their enthusiastic examples but her mind wasn't able to absorb another word, so sodden it was with information. The pile of catalogues grew to a teetering tower. She'd excelled at event planning when she was at school, having had to corral different personalities and needs, but nothing compared to this onslaught. Hours and hours later, Phee stood up from Aunt Cleo's desk and dragged herself to the door.

"Is there anyone else?" she called, unable to keep the fatigue from her voice.

She'd had nothing to eat during the siege of the funeral directors and the ewer of water she sipped from had long gone dry. The sitting room seemed empty as well, the hubbub of chatter now still, leaving an ambient silence as loud as a bee's hum.

A lone man waited in a darkened corner of the sitting room, untouched by sun or lamp. He stood to his impressive height at her words. She waved him inside the office and plunked herself down in the chair, indicated that he should sit across from her. To make up for the hours where she'd barely been able to get a word in, she began a light chatter, mostly about the carriage ride and the lovely, cozy house and how she'd had no idea there were so many options for casketry. The tower of brochures next to her began to wobble under its own weight but soon righted itself. Once the danger of it falling was over, she turned her attention for the first time to the man across the desk. Time slowed around her, allowing dust motes in the air to catch the last rays of sunshine to glisten like gems, and the world fell away, shrinking to only the two of them.

The mortician regarded Phaedra with care, listening with his entire self. It unnerved her, his focused gaze, his intensity. That intensity wasn't only in his eyes, it was in his nose: sleek and sharp, and in the shadows of his hollow cheeks.

Only his mouth escaped severity.

In the curves of that mouth, no, not a smile, he was much too professional for that. This was not a time for amusement. That curve was tender, welcoming, luring her to give over her secret emotions, silently announcing they would be safe with him, as he carried his own secrets, hidden to most but not to himself.

"I've never had to deal with this before." Phee spoke again to fill the stillness in the room and to calm the flutter in her chest. She flipped through an information packet from one of the earlier embalmers.

"All these burial plans, floor layouts, and orders of service complete with lists. The proper music for each facet of the service and the exact artist to perform each song, the proper incense to guide the dead on the path to the ever-lasting, the right food to serve at the repast," Phee fretted. She couldn't do this. She could barely get through a day of interviews. "It's overwhelming."

The mortician nodded, the planes of his cheekbones catching the rays of sunset. "I understand. I imagine you've had a full day." His voice was even, well-modulated like someone who spoke of horrific things often. He stood, and Phee was struck by how tall and thin he was. "If I may, I'll leave you with this. Please visit if you see fit."

He presented a card. On weighty white stock worthy of a grand ball invitation, the inky words stood out starkly. She ran her fingertip along the uncoated paper, feeling the fine grain and raised lettering:

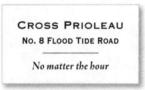

CROSS PRIOLEAU
No. 8 FLOOD TIDE ROAD

No matter the hour

Cross PRAY-low. She tasted the name. It was an old one, she could tell from its savor on her tongue. She also tasted her first name along with his last. Liking the combination too much, especially due to the improper timing, she moved on to the final words on his business card.

No matter the hour? That was certainly a departure from the other funeral directors, who had specific office hours emblazoned on their cards and brochures. Phee wondered if he made himself that available because business for him was slow. It had to be difficult, with the sheer amount of competition in this area. How could a town this size support them all?

Still, Phee said she would see all of the funeral directors before making a decision, and that was what she was going to do. The address meant nothing to her. She would have to find a map, or she could ask Mr. Prioleau for directions.

When she looked up from the card, he was gone. She hadn't heard him leave, but he'd left the faint fragrance of his aftershave tonic: cedar, rum, and immortelle flower.

TEN

Dinner was a welcome release from the incessant chatter of the day. Her body and mind were so leaden, she couldn't bring herself to stir even when she heard a door squeak, followed by the wind scuffing the curtains along the floor above her head and the creaking of copper pipes expanding. For a moment, she closed her eyes and absorbed the sounds of the house settling around her, grateful to not feel so alone.

Phee sat in front of the fireplace with food Zaye had hurriedly dropped by: chicken roasted with lemon and herbs and sliced over red rice, spicy pickled vegetables, and two generous slices of walnut pie, the top brittle-crisp and sandy over the fudgy, barely warm center. It was soul- and heartwarming food that restored her flagging energies and she ate heartily.

While she was grateful for the woman's kindness, she was happy to be left to her thoughts for the moment. Finished with her meal, she returned to the office. Ignoring the pile of papers from the funeral directors, Phee instead searched the desk drawers. Since that slow-to-a-crawl moment with Mr. Prioleau earlier, time had snapped back into place. The minutes ticked by, eating at Phee's resolve.

Zaye had expected her to have a funeral director selected already, and expressed her surprise when she had brought dinner that Phee hadn't even narrowed the list at all. She also had to admit she'd had no luck in finding any instructions from her aunt. Worry nibbled at her, thinking that Zaye might be the one Aunt Cleo chose to pomp her. Having another person take over was a humiliation unto itself. If that became the truth, Phee would have no choice but to surrender the pomp and go home. What would the law have to say about that? Maybe they would see it as a mishap, completely understandable in the circumstance and not an infraction that mandated punishment. Even if she managed to avoid jail, the scandal of having been accused would surely end her chances of gainful employment.

Bottles of green and black ink, several fountain pens, and a hand blotter lay in one drawer. In another, snowy writing paper and envelopes, embossed with Auntie Cleo's name underneath a raised image of a leafy fern—the stationery set she had given her. The next two were empty, while the final one held an embroidery ring, through which was fastened a square of ivory muslin cloth. A needle was pinned into a section of cloth outside the ring, done when the crafter took a break from the work. Within the hole of the needle was . . .

Phee peered closer, touched the thick thread to follow it to its source. She took the fine work from its place to see several spindles wrapped in what looked to be hair. A high-pitched cry escaped her. Then she gently lifted one of the spindles from its resting place. Indeed it was hair, dark and long. While it had been stretched over the wooden implement, the hair still retained some evidence that it had once been blessed with a corkscrew coil. Some was coal dark, other spindles held gray-white hair. Still others had been dyed into shades of green and pale blue to fit the artist's vision.

Reverently, she traced her fingers over the pattern on the cloth. It was incomplete, only the borders outlined in fine stitchings of hair. A large magnolia bud, just beginning to bloom, was stitched inside the middle of the embroidery loop. Ivory petals rouged a purpling pink at their base, hugging a tough center core. Each stitch was precise, tugged taut to form the intricate design. A bump of stitching fed into the loop itself, covered by the wooden bend and secured into place. Phee loosened the clasp holding the two pieces of the loop together and drew out the cloth. Beneath the flower bud were the words:

For Phaedra on her twenty-first year.

Aunt Cleo had not forgotten her. In all this time.

Farther into the recesses of the drawer was another piece of white cloth, this one folded into a square that would fit into the palm of her hand. Phee smoothed it out on her lap, careful not to disturb the fine needlework. This one was different, felt different. The design itself was a sheaf of ripe rice: long green stalks and leaves with their golden seed heads tenderly bowed, hewn straight by a stroke of the scythe. Harvest. Her aunt's full name was embroidered beneath the rice sheaf, along with the date of her birth and a dash to indicate only a date missing.

So Auntie Cleo had known she was going to die.

Phee held the cloth to her chest, her heart catching on the knowledge, tearing itself open. *Why didn't she tell the family? We would have—*

With a hiccough, Phee swallowed the bitter truth down. They would have done nothing. Mama's characteristic sourness would have only worsened her aunt's pain and isolation. And what if Mama turned her away? The chance Aunt Cleo would have received a warm welcome home in her final days was little to none, and Phee supposed living out her last in a place that cared for her was better than enduring blood relatives who didn't.

Guilt slid into her like the sharpest of knives, pushing up into her belly, twisting under her ribs. *You should have come before.* Phee dropped the fancywork back into the drawer. There was nothing she could do to change what had already occurred. The decisions or indecisions she'd made were over, and all she could do was live with the consequences. She could never apologize for not being present. All she could do now was give this final gift of her time and of herself.

Phee closed the drawer, stood with her palm pressed firm against her breastbone. She was sorry, so sorry. Despite her mother's unwelcome intrusions, Phee still suffered with loneliness over not finding any person she enjoyed spending time with, and angst that no career pursuits enchanted her at all. If she could have seen beyond Rosemount, she could have shared all that time with a wonderful person who had never allowed her to leave their thoughts.

She lurched back from the drawers, scraping the office chair against the polished floorboards and into the wall behind her. A frame nailed there joggled under the impact and rattled brokenly.

"Dag it," Phee muttered, moving to straighten the frame.

To her surprise, it wasn't a painting. It was a square wooden box, with a pane of glass on the face. Whatever was inside had slid off its mount and landed in the bottom of the box frame.

"Blast, blast, blast." Phee had intended to leave this house much as she had found it, in order for it to be sold, and breaking one of her aunt's items wasn't in that plan. With care, she lifted the display case from the wall to determine the damage she may have caused.

It struck her as she worked to remove the back panel holding in the contents: she hadn't thought of much beyond the pomp of arranging the homecoming service and burial. The removing of property from the house, selling it, settling her estate had not occurred to her. It didn't feel right to keep the money from the sale for herself. Maybe a charitable donation would suffice.

Finally, the back of the case slid away. Inside was a whole

blue crab shell, a female, judging by the apron on its belly. Many people used empty crab shells that had been cooked and picked clean for a variety of reasons. Her favorite was to serve deviled crab, a dish she loved, full of flaked white meat folded into sweet roasted onion and a sprinkle of powdered chili. Topped with herbed breadcrumbs baked to crispness. The telltale red-orange hue of the shell was a sign the creature had been cooked well.

But this crab retained the bright blue claws and olive-colored carapace it would have had in life, its sound hollow when Phee tapped it with her fingernail. How was that possible? A gentle shake revealed the creature rattled all on its ownsome, and the sound she'd heard was not its breaking.

Relieved, Phee investigated further, moving each of the five pairs of legs to no avail. Then she lifted the apron from the bottom of the beautiful, savory swimmer. Underneath where the gills known as dead man's fingers would be, well inside the she-crab's cavity, lay a key.

She drew it from its hiding place. Gold-tone in color, the key was the length of Phee's first finger and heavy for its size. What did it open? Immediately, she thought of the room with no means of entry. Would her bringing its key in close proximity to the door reveal a previously hidden access? Her head swung like she'd sampled one too many of Pop's creations and she perched on the edge of the desk, lest she fall. Surely a door with no opening was part and parcel of her imaginings of yesterday. Why would such a thing exist? She'd been overwrought after the argument with Mama and the journey, and with the added anticipation of the funeral directors arriving, it was no wonder her mind had taken to fancy.

Well . . . she would put those uncertainties to rest this moment and prove to herself once and for all that there was no dream door inside this house. She marched to the kitchen and took up the set of keys that lay in the hamper where she'd tossed them earlier, then headed up the stairs.

Only to find she had not been dreaming at all.

Phee stood in front of the final door at the end of the hall. It was without a keyhole, without hinges, but it radiated a cold so deep and endless, it burned. The keys fell from her hand. Beyond this door was something she didn't understand. Beyond this door was death. She was rooted to the spot, unable to turn away. Then, without any intention she could name, Phee threw herself at the door. Again and again and again. Thudding her body with all of her might against the unmoving surface. She thought perhaps she screamed. Something on her, in her, cracked. Like an egg thrown against a surface, she separated in twain, part of her sliding to the floor moments before the other half joined her.

She lay prone for countless moments, the ache in her head, neck, and shoulder in its own time bringing her back to the land of the living. Painfully, she rose from the floor, gathered the keys, and stood. Smoothed her skirts, then her hair. The moment of madness gone, she turned her back to the fourth door and headed across the hall, drinking in the preternatural calm filling her. She felt better. Much better. One by one, she tried the keys on the ring from Zaye. One by one they all failed to open the third door.

The final key on the ring slid without effort into the lock. With a click, the key turned completely around, sliding back the locking mechanism. The doorknob firm in her hand, she turned that, too, and the door swung wide.

A wave of air hit her face as she stood on the threshold, a mixture of cedar chest, camphor, and dust-covered drying roses. She sneezed, feeling along the wall for a light switch before entering the darkened room. Over the textured wallpaper she found it, and illumination from a lamp pierced the darkness. It did not chase it away completely, but gave Phee a path, a beacon to follow, and she entered.

Carpeting covered the floor in this room. The temperature of the air was warm, oh so warm, and she let the shawl fall from her shoulders. A bureau sat in one corner, a cedar chest in another. Paintings, none of them in frames, rested unhung against the far wall. Desert landscapes rendered in thick ochre with what looked like a blade from the sharp, raised edges. There were also fingerprints in the paint, like footsteps in the endless sand. In one painting, a distant swipe of sapphire blue haunted the upper corner. Later in the series of canvases, the blue swipe grew as it advanced, widening. In what Phee guessed were later renditions, the tools used improved. Or perhaps the painter's technique became more refined. The last paintings were devoid of the earlier angry slashes. The painter had become fond of the subject as it became more oasis than desert, capturing it with more tenderness.

All of it, however, whispered, *This time is past.* At the sole window to the room, movement. Phee's steps faltered.

A rustling in that corner penetrated the newborn calm within her. Gathering herself, she moved closer. Surely it had to be a bird or some small animal that had gotten inside this room through an open or broken window. But no, the window was intact and closed, covered with a heavy curtain usually reserved for winter months.

Rustling again. Phee crept closer to the sound, convincing herself it was a simple solution. A mouse, maybe. They were able to enter the smallest of spaces. She reached for the curtain. Before she could touch it the rustling came toward her, rushing, the sound blooming louder as it neared. Phee threw herself aside, and the sound passed by, headed toward the hallway, fading as it went.

Terror clutched her throat, suppressing the shriek that bubbled to her lips. That sound had brought the sensation of being in the path of something or someone determined to get by, even if they must go through you to do so. It was enough to dispel any lingering calm residing within her. But she had seen nothing. Her heart was in her throat and her breath came in pants like she'd run at full tilt. She couldn't run now. Her legs were water and she sank down onto the rug, her head in her hands.

Alone. You are alone in this house. No one will come to help you. Though harsh, the thought rallied her. And she crawled along the carpet on her hands and knees until she reached a chair she could press her back against. There was nowhere else she could go. If she left here, and returned home with her tail tucked, in all likelihood to serve time behind iron bars, she would never be able to hold her head up again. If she even survived the horrid conditions in the prison, it would be a scandal that would live on in St. Margaret folklore, bandied about at every wedding, funeral, and family event. If the family could ostracize her aunt for stealing a necklace, what fate awaited her?

Would that be such a bad thing? she wondered. As she hadn't located any instructions, it was possible Auntie Cleo wanted Zaye to pomp for her in the first place. Why not allow the woman, who clearly loved her aunt, to handle the proceedings? There was a simple solution: turn everything over to Zaye, go home, and announce it was done. That she had completed the task in record time, with success, and Mama may never be the wiser. But even if Zaye kept the secret, Phee herself would know that Mama had been right and Phee had not been able to manage the duty of pomp. And that secret would haunt the rest of her life.

Yes, she was alone, but that didn't mean she was helpless. She'd promised to meet with all of the funeral directors, and she would keep that promise. Tomorrow, she would go to see Mr. Prioleau and from that point make her choice—admitting her lack of knowledge but embracing her determination to do the right thing. She leaned her head against the chair, the texture of the seat covering rough against her cheek. *People do strange things when they're deep in grief,* Pop had said. Why should she be any different?

Heartened by her decision, Phee got to her knees and made her way over to the cedar chest. It met her mid-thigh when she'd stood next to it, but now it was at her breast. Walnut-colored like herself, the chest was covered with a white linen cloth, edged in a spidery lace. She tugged at one corner of the fabric and it smoothed away over the polished surface beneath. Mama had one exactly like this, and Phee wondered if this was a ritual she would have to practice again one day.

The chest was locked. Phee drew out the gold-tone key and it fit, releasing a rush of cedar, rosemary, and clove. The lid held the name of the company that had manufactured the chest and the date it was founded: *Lanier, 1745.* Reverently, Phee investigated the contents.

Old documents, fragile and tea-stained by time. Programs from plays where her aunt and her mother had performed tied to folded costumes, the fabric gone crisp with age. Marks her aunt had gotten over her school years, along with scrawled notes from teachers stating Cleo was good with her lessons, but was such a quiet, solitary child. It was a concern and she needed to be drawn out to become more social like her younger sister, who was a delight. Phee pressed her lips together and replaced the grading cards.

There was sheet music for piano and a small recorder in a burgundy-colored case. But there was no sheet music for that instrument. Wrapped inside tissue paper was a pale pink tea dress with low-heeled satin slippers dyed to match. Phee recognized the outfit. It was the one Aunt Cleo had worn to Mama's wedding. A portrait of the family on that momentous occasion had pride of place at Rosemount. The clothes had been packed away with care, but sadness clung to the fabric, and Phee hurriedly replaced them.

Looking deeper, she found a large envelope, its middle plump with contents. The words "final papers" were scrawled along the front in a trembling hand. Phee couldn't believe her luck. She unwound the string from around the cardboard button on the reverse side and drew out the papers inside, her own hands trembling.

Her joy was short-lived. As she read through the materials inside, she realized they were written by her grandmother and named Cleonine as pomp. But hadn't Mama done the homegoing service for her grandmother? It was the family lore she had grown up with—that Gran had named Madelyn as her pomp and Mama had worked and planned to give her the grandest send-off possible, exactly as she'd wanted. One of the most well-attended and well-received homegoings the city had ever seen. Why had Mama lied?

You are a liar!

The memory of Aunt Cleo staring at Mama over Phee's head and enunciating those words shook her to her core. At the time, it had been the only sticking point of the argument where she had leaned toward her mother's side. Madelyn St. Margaret was a lot of things, but she always told the truth, no matter how difficult. Between this new information and the falsehood to dissuade Phee from taking this pomp, she had never known her mother to stretch the truth. She'd been concerned about her lack of knowledge of Aunt Cleo. Now she wondered if she truly knew her own mother.

Phee flipped through more of the envelope's contents. Auntie had clearly taken her responsibility seriously. There were logs on the dates and times she had taken the presentations of the morticians, and notes on their services. Even Cross Prioleau was listed—he must have been quite a young man at the time—but his name was struck out so violently the paper was sliced through as if the person had used a knife.

Auntie had even created her own program for the order of services, written in her florid script. But her original copy looked nothing like the one Phee had taken from the drawer in the hallway. The image of Gran on the front was different, as was the music, the passages of scripture; none of it matched. Truth now—one thing had not changed: the pallbearers. All names she recognized as uncles, or cousins, or people so close to the family they might as well be kin. Why did it change?

She flipped back through the log of funeral directors, skimming the pages until she got to Mr. Prioleau's. A scrawl in the margin that looked uncannily like her mother's writing proclaimed him "odd."

Was being an oddity enough to exclude someone from

performing a homegoing, or did her mother know something at the time about the man that made him unsuitable? Had he been run out of New Charleston because of his supposedly odd manner? Or did the reason go deeper—perhaps into some unsavory business practices? If Phee chose Mr. Prioleau as funeral director, would that decision find its way back to New Charleston, and if it did, was he so unsuitable that solely the decision to employ him would place her in violation of Auntie Cleo's pomp? If Mama questioned her choices, Phee had the original documents showing her mother had taken over Grandma's pomp from Auntie Cleo and could brandish them in front of the entire family for her own defense. But if the law questioned it, what could she say to prevent them from dragging her off? Being taken to jail was unacceptable. When Phee left Rosemount, it would be on her terms, not because she was forced out—either by her mother or the law.

If Phee had not already decided to call on Mr. Prioleau first thing in the morning, this certainly would have turned her mind to it. She had to speak with him to see what kind of person he was and how he conducted his business before finalizing anything. Her mind firmly set, Phee slid her fingernail into the slit in the paper from the strike of a metal pen nib, the severed edges frayed soft.

Of course, there could be a sensible explanation of why the pomp transferred from sister to sister. Aunt Cleo could have been ill or incapacitated due to her own grief.

She could have asked Mama to handle the pomp for her. So many avenues to explore and so little time. She twirled the string that closed the envelope in her fingers. Aunt Cleo's body was waiting, and the dead did not like to wait. The longer the body lingered, the longer Phee stayed in this house courting madness.

ELEVEN

Phee awoke before the sun, determined to fulfill her promise. She had to meet with Cross Prioleau, the final mortician on the list Zaye had so thoughtfully provided. The clock on the wall struck five times. Was it so early? The house had its own soft natural light, enough to see by, making it a challenge to determine the hour of the day.

She washed and dressed with leisure, not wanting to leave the house too early. But after a cup of tea and one of Zaye's tender breakfast rolls, the clock had not struck the hour again. Images of Mr. Spring's photography surfaced in her mind's eye and she could see each and every discolored face again.

Who did the body?

Her stomach turned over and she quickly finished her tea to settle it. She picked up the business card from the kitchen table where she'd left it. *No matter the hour,* it said. *Well,* Phee thought, draping the shawl around her shoulders, *we will see if you hold to your word.*

Horizon was still quiet in the early hours of the morning, where droplets of dew clung to the shrubs cordoning off each home's front garden from the sleek black path. The air was fresh, as if it had rained, even though Phee had not heard any during the night. It was a revelation to hear her heels clicking solidly on the path. At home, she would only walk on the elevated wooden esplanades that ran the entire length of the city, and the sound her shoes made was much more muffled. Hollow, almost. She marveled at the difference between the careful steps necessary on the springy esplanades against the ones she could make here: firm, solid, stead—

"Ohh!"

Her attention on her feet, Phee had failed to look where she was going and bumped into another early riser strolling down the path. The woman was older, much older than even her mother, her back humped within her shabby coat as though she were protecting herself from a cold, biting wind.

"Watch where you going! Stupid girl," the woman said. "Like I ain't got enough wrong without some hoity gal running me down in the street."

"My mind was elsewhere, ma'am. I am sincerely sorry." Phee attempted to help the woman but she shrank away from her offered hand.

Instead, the woman brandished her cane in Phee's face, shaking it threateningly enough that Phee recoiled. "You sure should be sorry! Trampling me underfoot like it's nothin'." She looked Phee over from the top of her pomaded updo, secured with mother-of-pearl combs, to the tips of her polished boots. "Suppose I am to you."

Phee gaped, unable to stop herself. Aside from her mother, no one had ever spoken to her in such a manner. She recalled Auntie Cleo's letter filled with details of her helping people displaced by the war, those who had lost everything, including their families and their livelihood. After a stupefied moment, she found her voice.

"Of course, I don't believe that. I can only offer my apologies, ma'am. Shall I call a doctor for you? I will pay for it. My aunt's house is just up the road." She paused, realizing she had no idea if she could do such a thing as send a messenger for a doctor in Horizon. She was operating without thought, not keeping in mind she was the visitor here and did not know the way the town operated.

The woman squinted at Phee. "Up the road where?"

Phee told her.

"Cleonine's house? Cleo is your aunt?" Before Phee could acknowledge this fact, the woman grunted and moved away, leaning on her cane. "You ain't nothing like Cleo Simons. Sure is a shame."

Bewildered, Phee watched her hobble away, off toward whatever destination had brought her out this early in the morning. She blinked against the rise of guilt in her breast. No, she wasn't Cleo Simons. Auntie Cleo would have never let this much time pass before seeing Phee, if she'd been able to. Auntie Cleo had made her own way in life when her own family turned their backs on her. So she had tried to take an heirloom from the house. It wasn't as if they didn't have plenty of them and Aunt Cleo didn't deserve a keepsake of her own mother.

Phee continued down the street a ways, this time watching the path in front of her. A couple, not much older than herself, were walking arm-in-arm down the opposite side of the street. They smiled with what seemed like invitation and Phee quickened her steps to join them. As she approached, the woman—eyes sparkling with sympathy—spoke like they were old friends.

"We saw what happened. Don't you mind Ol' Miss Johnson. She is the same to everyone—surly and downright ornery."

Old Miss Johnson? Aunt Cleo never mentioned her in any letters. "I am glad to know it . . . I suppose." Phee laughed. "At the very least, I have comfort that it is not my presence alone that offends her."

"No, it is the presence of anyone excepting herself," the young gentleman said with a good-natured chuckle.

They made introductions and Phee expressed her pleasure to meet the Cooks: Wilbur and Ann. Like many freedmen and women, they wore clothing made from disused Union uniforms. It seemed Mrs. Ann was a magician with the new Singer sewing machines; she had cleverly made a beautiful shirtwaist from the blue fabric and paired it with a vivid skirt in a mauveline shade. As for her husband, he sported a gray sack jacket and matching trousers.

"My apologies for interrupting your stroll, but I was wondering if you knew where I can find this address." Phee held out the card, but Ann hesitated to take it from her hand. The sparkle left her eyes and her gaze flicked away and down.

"It's all right, Annie," her husband said gently. "You can do it. Like we practiced."

Wide-eyed, Phee watched as Ann took the card from her hand. With great care, she sounded out the words of Mr. Prioleau's name as if saying them for the first time.

"I know my numbers easy," she said, and read it off. The rest of the card was slow going as well, but Ann Cook managed to pronounce it all correctly with a little help from her husband. When she finished, she beamed and it was as if the clouds had parted. "I did it!"

"You sure did! See? Wasn't nothing to be afraid of." Wilbur squeezed her hands. "She's still learning her reading. Miss Simons was helping her before she passed."

"Oh, she was wonderful." Ann returned the card to Phee. "Never made me feel the least bit bad that I never learned before."

"Wasn't your fault you wasn't allowed to learn, Annie."

It struck Phee then. "Oh! Oh . . . I'm so sorry. I—I . . ." Her words faded away, inadequate to express her horror and sorrow.

But Ann pressed a gloved hand to Phee's. "It's gonna be all right now. Don't you worry."

"I can help you. With . . . with your reading. Miss Simons was my aunt. I'm here to see to her homegoing."

Wilbur removed his hat, holding it to his chest. "I am truly sorry for your loss. It's a loss to the whole town. She made this place what it is."

"We thank you for the offer, but we stayed here long enough to get on our feet, and we'll be heading off first thing on tomorrow." Ann's eyes sparkled with tears this time. "If we could stay for her services, we would. But we have train tickets for the morning."

Tears prickled Phee's eyes as well. Maybe the Cooks could have been friends to her, in this place of the unfamiliar. She could have helped Ann with her transition from enslaved person to freed woman. Helped her learn to read. The four of them could have had lovely dinners together, talking long into the evening, if she had just visited Auntie Cleo earlier. Now it was too late . . . for so many things. She smiled tightly, holding back her regret. Her jaw thumped with pain.

"Oh, I almost forgot. You were looking for Cross's place." Wilbur gave Phee directions and wished her well, while Ann gave her an impromptu embrace.

"I know we don't know each other at all, but I couldn'ta stopped myself if I tried. I just feel so—"

"Free?"

Ann nodded while Wilbur gazed at her with such tenderness it made Phee's throat constrict. "We must go, Miss Phaedra."

"Please call me Phee. For when you write and tell me how you both are. You can use my aunt's address. It can be sent to me wherever I am." She was so loath to see them go.

"We will!" Ann replied, and she and Wilbur strolled away, waving.

Phee realized when they were spots in the distance that she hadn't thanked them for giving her directions. "Oh, Phaedra. Where is your head?"

She crossed the street and headed for the path to Flood Tide Road at a brisk pace, pulling her aunt's shawl closer around her shoulders. An early rising gardener hailed her politely as she walked, and she nodded in return. Both Abbot and Mr. Facey had said the dead don't want to hang around on the side of the living for too long. She had accepted it as truth, but what did it mean for her and this service she was planning? Phee rubbed the bruise blossoming on her shoulder from where she'd hit against the fourth door and winced. She was grateful to have not bruised her face. Was her aunt's spirit angry, vengeful at her delay? No matter what happened, she needed to make the right decision, not just a hasty one.

After about ten minutes, the path steadily rose toward a stone building in the distance. Phee huffed out a breath. "Wish I'd worn my traveling trousers."

She found the climb less strenuous than she'd imagined, her attention having been taken by several intricate tombstones lining both sides of the path. Not one of them was alike. A few were taller than she was, one or two were heartachingly tiny. Marble of white and gray dominated, but she saw sparks of pink and green and blue among the sea of memorials. The fragrance of cypress hovered in the air that blew salt across her lips. She licked them, and hurried the last few lengths to the stone building.

It was a modest place, but sturdy. Built to last. She strode around, looking for the front door. A bird warbled as she raised her hand to knock, capturing her attention for the briefest moment, and she dropped her hand, turning fully to watch it perch on the branch of a nearby pine, then run across to its nest.

"Miss St. Margaret?"

The voice behind her was closer than she'd expected and Phee gasped as she spun around to face it. "Goodness! I about leapt out of my skin!" Her heart thudded like a trapped thing. Magician's mercy, she was all nerves.

Cross Prioleau stood in the doorway, a magnifying loupe nestled against the ridge of his eye socket. He removed it before addressing her again.

"Apologies for startling you."

He was dressed less formally today, in his shirtsleeves and heavy broadcloth trousers instead of the three-piece she'd met him in. It suited his spare frame. His sleeves were rolled up to the elbow, revealing arms of a strength she had not imagined he possessed. She had to look up to see his face, and it gave her the impression of gazing up at a mountain. His clean-shaven jawline caught the rising morning light and she sank her fingers into the spaces of the shawl in an effort not to touch his cheek. His voice was the same calm tone she remembered from yesterday and she began to feel more at ease.

"No, it's . . . I'm all right." She loosened her grip on the shawl, touched her fingertips to her temple. "It's only that I've been awake for ages and your card said no matter the hour and I am in all likelihood too early."

"Not at all. Please come in." He stepped back and gestured for her to follow him.

Phee did, to a worktable in his front room. Though the

table was set in front of a large open window, a squash-neck lamp bent over it.

"Would you like a drink?"

"Another time, perhaps."

He waited for her to speak even though he would have been well within his rights to ask the reason for her visit. The memory of Mr. Spring's photographic efforts had been strong this morning when she started out from Aunt Cleo's, but now they were fading with speed. Phee cast her gaze around the tidy house again, noting the sparse furnishings were clean and in good repair. She sensed he was a careful man, a patient one, completely at ease with himself and what he had to offer. He'd waited to speak with her yesterday, and when he'd taken note of her overburdened state, had left any further contact to her devices.

"Were you making jewelry?" she asked, indicating the loupe.

"Not exactly." He pulled out a chair, placed it close enough for her to see.

On the table, resting on cotton bedding, was an egg. She'd never seen one so distinctive before—pale blue-green with a paint-spatter pattern of brown and gray. No longer than her pinkie finger, the shell had a crack, and a chip was missing from its surface.

Phee was saddened to see the damage. "Oh, it's broken."

"Not for much longer." Cross replaced the loupe to his eye, donned a pair of gloves, and bent to work.

Fascinated, Phee watched while he carefully swabbed near the broken surfaces with a liquid she recognized as one for cleaning wounds. The crack, he repaired with the thinnest paintbrush touched to a clear glue. The missing chip took more consideration. Cross opened the box next to him—it was full of shell fragments from various birds. Patterns of red-brown on ivory, olive with off-white speckled, and some colored like the broken one in front of him.

He chose a piece, held it over the missing space. A slight shake of his head and the piece returned to the box. He chose another, turning it several times to see if the pattern would match. When it pleased him, he then took up a slim pair of scissors and trimmed the shell patch to fit the egg. The barest touch of the adhesive and Phee could not tell where the chip had been.

"Marvelous!" she exclaimed, applauding. "Especially for something no bigger than a thimble. What will you do with it now?"

Cross sat back, removed the loupe, and packed away his tools. "Return it to its nest."

"It's still alive?"

"Yes, I hope so. I've kept it warm under this light." He stood and placed the delicate life on its cushion of cotton into a box. "I'll have to be quick, if you'd like to wait for me here."

"I'd like to accompany you, if that's all right."

"More than."

Phee didn't begin conversation on the way to the tree. This felt like too much of a moment for idle chatter. To add to that, she didn't want to break the focused concentration Cross showed. He asked her to bear the box while he approached the fork of a tree where a nest lay. The rustling of leaves was the only chorus while Cross climbed a stepladder, his impressive height requiring he only ascend one rung. He gestured and Phee raised the box above her head like an offering, and Cross removed the egg and returned it to its home.

"Quickly now," he said, gathering the stepladder. "Before Mother returns." The pair made their way back to the house.

"That was outstanding." Phee clapped her hands, beaming. "Invigorating, even. I've never seen such a thing."

"I'm pleased to have shown you."

Cross removed his gloves, turned his full attention to Phee as he did the first time they met. A flutter in her belly accompanied the strange wash of heat along her collar. At the same moment he opened his mouth to speak again, the sound of galloping hooves took their attention away from each other to gaze at a fast-approaching rider.

TWELVE

The ground beneath Phee and Cross shook with the vibration of the large bay's approach. Wide-eyed, the rider pulled up his mount a few feet away from the pair. He dismounted, holding the horse loosely by the reins, and approached. Beside her, Phee could feel the normally serene man tense.

"Cross Prioleau?" he said, striding toward them.

"I am he."

"Doc Solomon is sending for you. They've found another. Will you come?"

"Tell him I'm on my way."

The messenger agreed even as he swung into the saddle. He was galloping away before Phee could catch her breath.

"I'm sorry, Miss St. Margaret. But I must go. If you would like, I will come to you when I return." He headed toward the barn. His words jolted Phee out of her inaction and she rushed to follow his long strides.

"Are you going to a job? Please . . . let me come with you."

He pulled the barn door open, then began tacking up a

horse. His sure movements wasted no extra motion. It was beautiful to watch the competency with which he worked.

"They have called me to do an easing." He looked directly into her eyes. Into her. "Are you sure you want to see such?"

Flashes of Mr. Smiley's photographs plagued her: still, painful-looking bodies that should have been and felt at rest. Seeing the images had haunted her and she'd known there had to be another way. Perhaps Mr. Prioleau could show her that.

Phee took a deep breath, steeling herself. Time was short. She wasn't afraid of jail or even her mother's wrath at this moment. More important were her aunt's wishes, and in the absence of those, her own dedication to trying to make up for her own absence from her beloved aunt's life. "I am sure. To do this pomp justice, I will endure anything."

He nodded, leading the horse to a sturdy trap. The small carriage was built for two and he attached the horse's saddle to the harness, making sure to gently pull its tail out from under the breeching, then attaching the breastplate, collar, and driving bit. It would have been faster for him to refuse her and ride off on his single mount, but he had taken the extra time to prepare the carriage.

"Thank you," she said as he handed her inside.

He nodded. "It will be a brisk ride and not a smooth one. But I'll be as careful as I can."

"I'm not a fragile eggshell, Mr. Prioleau. Drive as you will so we can get there soonest."

His slight smile warmed her more than the sun cresting

into the rising morning. He clicked his tongue to the horse and they were away. As they drove, she turned to glance at his profile.

"I appreciate your allowing me to come with, Mr. Prioleau."

"Pleased for your company," he said, lightly flicking the reins. "Be better pleased if you'd call me Cross."

While it was early in their acquaintance for that, Phee agreed and offered her own first name. Recognizing the significance of abandoning the accepted formality, they both fell into a comfortable silence. The trap hit one wheel against a rock embedded in the road and it jostled the carriage up on the right side where Phee sat. With a squeak of surprise, Phee slid into Cross, banging into his side. She grasped his arm to right herself, gasping at his sheer solidity. He looked so rangy and spare, she hadn't suspected to find him in such good trim.

"Okay?" he asked, glancing at her with concern.

"Yes, fine." Heat rushed to her face and she twined her hands in her lap. *Magician's mercy,* she thought.

The journey took the better part of an hour, longer than it would have taken a single rider on horseback, but Cross reassured her the additional time was of no matter. When they entered the hospital and descended the stairs behind a harried doctor into the chilled darkness of the basement morgue, Phee understood why. She stood next to Cross, watching the gaslight flicker around the room, creating shadows and deepening the existing darkness that lingered in corners. Unsettled, she folded her hands in front of her, surreptitiously holding on to a bit of her skirt in case she needed to lift it to bolt back up the stairs.

As if sensing her discomfiture, Cross gave her his tender not-quite-a-smile. "I would be grateful for your help today, Phee."

Hearing her chosen moniker from him brought back the reasons she had asked to be here. None of the other funeral directors had offered this experience to her, and she would be a fool not to take it. Slowly, she released the fabric and it fell back into place.

"Whatever I can do."

Cross nodded, then addressed their escort. "Dr. Solomon, this is Phee St. Margaret, my assistant for today."

The doctor acknowledged her with a nod before donning spectacles and reading from the board clip in his hands. "Same as last time, Mr. Prioleau. Since the Thirteenth Amendment passed, those who aren't happy to lose what they still consider their property have been taking matters into their own hands. Seems some haven't even told those poor people they're free under the law now."

Dr. Solomon pulled back a curtain to reveal a table covered with a white sheet. Phee blinked, narrowed her eyes to see it more clearly. She couldn't understand what could be under that cloth. The form it made was crude, misshapen, inconceivable.

"Some of our people up North took in a young man, a runaway about eighteen or so," Dr. Solomon continued. "Recently, he disappeared. Turns out his former owner tracked him down and packed him in a crate to take back to his plantation. Old coot was spitting mad, saying he didn't care what the law was, that boy was his. Wouldn't tell a soul where he was. Once the search party finally found the young man, well . . ."

The doctor indicated the sheet. Phee pressed her fingers over her mouth as Cross went over to the table and took up the cloth in both hands. She gasped as he tugged it, and the sheet slid away.

Upon the table was the body. He was no boy, but a young man nonetheless. Curled in on himself as if he were trying to avoid blows hitting him. His fingers, what she could see of them, were skeletal as claws. Fear, sadness, and an ultimate lack of hope were engraved into his final expression. On one side of his face, an ashy line that Phee recognized as a streak of dried tears marred the brown cheek.

"Oh, mercy."

This was the first time she'd seen anger in Cross. His jaw worked, the gaslight from the overhead lamps carving deep into the hollows of his cheekbones. Ramrod-straight back and shoulders, a far cry from his earlier stance. He closed his eyes, breathed deep and slow before opening them again.

"Do you want to preserve the clothes?" he asked.

"Preserve everything you're able to," the doctor replied as he placed the chart on an empty examination table, then turned toward the stairs. "For the courts."

"Aren't you going to help us, Doctor?" Phee called to him.

He shook his head, then patted Cross firmly on the

shoulder. "No, miss. Cross is the knowledgeable one here. My duty is to the living, not the dead." A brisk nod. "Good luck and good day."

Phee watched him ascend the stairs, unable to stop comparing the departing doctor to Desmond. While they had similar professions, she couldn't imagine Dr. Desmond Sweet even acknowledging the talents of anyone besides himself. He was selfish, focused only on his own needs, and could be cruel in the pursuit of attaining them. Also, he was a great believer in the silence and subservience of women. She shuddered to think what being wed to him would mean.

Now was not the time for such thoughts, Phee chastised herself before glancing at the young man on the table. While the dark damp of this morgue unnerved her, this was no time to have thin resolve. Cross had introduced her as his assistant and she would be exactly that.

"What do we do now?" Phee unwrapped one of the peanut candies in her pocket and slipped the treat in her mouth, the sugar bolstering her.

Cross sighed, letting his anger dissipate. "Please look at the chart and tell me the deceased's name, if it is there."

While she sucked on the candy, Phee crossed the room, thinking that she was doing Desmond a disservice. Not every doctor functioned the same. It was likely Desmond had never even encountered a deceased person like this, so how would she know how he would react? She picked up the chart and flipped through the pages. And thinking him selfish? Cruel? Ambitious, more like. For once, why couldn't she just accept—

Phee froze, the pages on the board clip fluttering to stillness. These ideas about Desmond weren't her own. They were her mother's. She spat the candy into her handkerchief, wiped her tongue. The lingering sweetness sickened her. A compulsion spell. Never would she have believed her own mother would hex her into anything she didn't want to do. Especially not marriage. But she had underestimated her mother's ambition. Apparently, it rivaled Desmond's.

"Phee?" Cross's gentle query nudged her. "Are you all right?"

Her head jerked up. "Yes, perfectly well." She cleared her throat. "It says his name is—was—Elijah. No age is recorded."

"That's fine." Cross stood at the end of the table where Elijah lay curled into a ball. He gently tried to straighten the boy's limbs, but dying in that enclosed box had kept him in this cramped form.

"My name is Cross Prioleau and you have been found, Elijah."

Phee did not know what to expect, but she certainly did not think Cross would begin talking directly to the deceased. His voice was gentle as Phee was used to, but it also vibrated with a certain power that she could not name or recall hearing before.

"You are safe now." He placed his hand on the bare skin of the young man's ankle. "No longer alone. Instead you are here with friends."

Phee stared as Cross moved around the table, laying hands on the body, uncaring about her mouth staying open in shock.

"You have been found, Elijah, and we can tell your family where you are. Your friends as well." Cross smiled as he spoke and it infused his reassuring words. "I'm sure they never gave up hope. Never gave up searching for you."

His hands were on the young man's shoulder when she saw the crook in Elijah's back begin to straighten. She gasped, her heart ringing like a hammer striking iron. The more Cross spoke, the more the stiffened, crooked joints calmed, eased out of their tortured state. When Phee was able to pull her gaze from Elijah, Cross motioned her over to the table. She held her breath as she headed toward them.

"Only if you are comfortable," Cross whispered as she joined him at Elijah's side. "Introduce yourself."

Slowly, Phee rubbed her lips together, deciding. She knew Cross would never judge her if she chose to leave the room or hover in the corner while he worked. But she didn't want to do that. Not now. She believed this was a matter the Freedman's Bureau should know about, and she wanted to tell her father. Maybe he could do something. But not now. Now it was time for *her* to do something.

"Hello. I'm Phee St. Margaret, Elijah." Trembling, she slid her hand under his, allowing his cool, stiff fingers to rest on her warm ones. Gooseflesh rose on her arms and up the back of her neck.

She had no idea what to say to this person who had

known more pain than she ever had. Who had tasted freedom, then been hunted and captured only to die alone in a crate, where he'd been destined for more evil. Phee thought of what she would have wanted to say to Aunt Cleo if she'd had the chance. If she had been able to see her, talk with her one more time. She cleared her throat, dry now that the effects of the candy were no more.

"I'm here. You're no longer alone. Cross and myself, we are here. Here to . . . help. So you . . . um, so you can be at peace." She looked to Cross and he nodded.

"Help us help you, friend," Cross murmured. "We have some of our people telling your family where you are. I'm sure you will want to go with them when they arrive. Let us get you ready."

For what felt like hours, they spoke to Elijah. Not only did his limbs ease, the expression on his face gentled as well. It was like he was finally at peace. His face looked as Phee was used to seeing the dead at homegoings—as if they were sleeping soundly.

Her back ached from leaning over Elijah and her stomach protested her lack of nourishment, but inside Phee was triumphant. When Cross told her the next steps in cosseting the body, she was only too happy to assist.

THIRTEEN

The pair left the morgue through a back doorway that led into a small courtyard. After so long under gas lamps, Phee squinted in the afternoon sunlight. She shuddered, rubbing her arms under her shawl as her skin warmed. Funny how she hadn't felt the cold once the corpse easing had begun. As Phee and Cross ascended the stone steps, he asked after her.

"Well?"

"I have never in my life spent a more challenging and worthwhile day." It was woefully inadequate to describe her experience.

"I am glad," he said, handing her into the carriage. "Your help was invaluable."

She shook her head. "I did nothing."

"On the contrary, you were a natural. The young man responded to your earnest tone." The carriage dipped slightly as he climbed in beside her and took up the reins. "Alone, the entire affair would have taken me much longer. Thank you."

Thrilled at his compliment, Phee pressed back into the

carriage seat. This was the most he'd spoken to her since they'd met, and she suspected he might wish to remain quiet for a fair portion of the drive, to be with his thoughts. Likewise, she held the events of the past few hours close to her chest.

Tears clogged her throat as she relived the effects of the young man's horrific last moments melting away under Cross's reassuring words. And possibly her own. Mr. Spring's photographs had disgusted her when she'd believed them to only be a product of his own ignorance and lack of skill. Now she knew better. Now she was aware of what those cramped hands and eternal grimaces meant; she understood the horror those photographs truly held. She looked at her fingers, recalling how Elijah's hand had relaxed and softened into her own, until it rested in hers like a trusting child's.

Cross set a slower pace this time—as leisurely as Abbott had for her arrival—the carriage gently rocking like a cradle. His quiet nature allowed her to be alone with the feelings in her heart as they journeyed back to Horizon.

Phee wound her fingers into the shawl's openwork wool and pulled it closer around her as the countryside trundled past. This morning when she'd arrived at Cross Prioleau's home, her intention had been to ask him how he would approach her aunt's final show of care. She had expected a prepared speech or presentation in a similar vein to those from the other funeral directors. Instead, she had experienced his work in the most intimate way possible.

The man had repaired a damaged eggshell when most

others would never have noticed it broken to start, much less taken the time to learn such a skill. And the corpse easing . . . she was still in awe of his abilities in that. Mama might find him odd, but there was much Mama found odd about Phee herself. The notes she'd found of her mother's had been written ten years ago, although they felt as though they were from another age altogether.

Now that Phee knew her mother was willing to hex her own daughter to get her way, any trust or reverence for her opinion had blown away like so much dust. There was no one else she trusted more than herself, her own heart and mind. From what she had seen today, Cross would support her in each and every decision. She would be proud to answer the question about who did the body with his name.

"Pardon me, Mr. Prioleau . . ."

"Cross," he offered.

Phee smiled, even as she twisted her hands in her lap. "Cross. I came to you this morning to ask if you had a presentation for me, some indication of your work before I made my decision as pomp for my aunt. But I have seen all I need to today."

She took a deep breath, hoping she remembered the proper words. "Cross Prioleau, I offer you the position of funerary director for Cleonine Simons, should you wish to accept it."

That small curve of the lip showed itself. "It is my honor to accept and will be my honor to execute your wishes."

Phee acknowledged with a nod, keeping her gaze on

the road ahead. Something hummed within Cross, not unlike what she'd felt earlier during the easing. It frizzled along her skin as well, taking her good sense with it. Then his reply registered with her.

"*My* wishes—not my aunt's?"

"I am aware you haven't found your aunt's instructions yet." At that, her head snapped toward him, but he regarded her without rancor. "It is the way of living in a small place like Horizon. Word spreads quickly."

Phee let out an exasperated breath. "Especially if it is not a good word?"

"Exactly that."

She set her jaw, ready to argue her point. "I can do this."

"I know."

Cross's quiet voice once again disarmed her. His hands were clasped on the reins, his shoulders pulled back and down, and for all the spareness of his frame Cross managed to fill the space between them. Phee had left an appropriate distance, and he had respected it. Even so, his presence seemed to draw closer to her, nudging away the weighty guilt and loneliness that tore at her.

"Two things, if you will."

He was her advisor in this process now. "Go on."

"Have you opened the curtains in the house? The windows?"

After a moment's thought, Phee realized she hadn't. She enjoyed the coziness of the house, the feeling of being safely cradled in its embrace. "No, I haven't. Is there a reason I should?"

Cross nodded once. "The recently deceased frequently need instruction as to how to move on. They tend to keep their old routines and patterns until shown the path out."

Phee's mouth opened, then closed. She fussed with the button on one of her gloves. "Are you saying my aunt needs help understanding that she is deceased?"

"As many dead do." He watched her machinations a moment then brought his gaze back to her face. "This causes one to often see and hear things as the deceased goes about their daily business."

Phee worked the button back and forth in its hole. The pea-sized button popped free and Phee caught it with a soft cry, hurriedly dropping it into a pocket. Perhaps that explained the . . . odd occurrences she'd met in the house. "And the other thing?"

"Perhaps you could choose the clothes your aunt should wear. Or locate an image of her for a certain hairstyle she might prefer."

"Start small, you are saying?"

"It is hardly small, but it is a start."

Phee tucked the gloves away, smoothed her skirt. "A good one, I think."

Light crawled across the sky, heading for early evening, and the murmur of Horizon greeted them. As they reached the hilltop overlooking Cross's home and place of business, he pointed out that he had a visitor. A lone crow approached the nest where he had placed the repaired egg. After a short circuit of the area, it settled into the nest, letting out a content rattle. Phee finally saw his full smile and it warmed her more than the sunlight. "Would you like to come in for supper?"

"I should go," Phee said, reluctant. "So much to do and I am eager to begin."

"Of course." He drove her to the door of her aunt's home, where she alighted without assistance. "I will call on you tomorrow afternoon."

"I look forward to it."

In truth, Phee did not begin until the next morning. She had known her mother was hardheaded with her intentions, but Phee hadn't expected her to go to this length to exert her control. After throwing out the remaining candies and partaking in a hearty meal of Zaye's provisions to help rid her system of Mama's hex, she was too physically shattered to begin searching through her aunt's belongings. With hope Zaye had meant her no ill when bringing her food, Phee went to bed early on a full belly and slept deeply.

Awaking with the sun, full of energy and intent, Phee prepared herself for a busy day. She knew the clothes, knew the hairstyle for her aunt's last. The mirror had shown her. It would be the blue chiffon dress Auntie Cleo had been wearing in the orchard when she looked so happily, so lovingly at someone Phee was unable to see. Her dark coils brushed and smoothed with soft pomade into an upsweep. The metallic shawl draped around her shoulders.

The shawl she would have trouble parting with. It had become such a comfort to her in such a short time, providing just the right amount of warmth and giving Phee something to hold on to when her nerves got the better of her. This was only her fourth day of being here in Horizon. While she was still under pressure, the frantic race of her heart, the throb behind her eye had lessened. She pulled the handwoven material closer around her shoulders, removed the dress from the closet, and laid it on the rocker.

Cross had said to choose her clothing from the skin out, so Phee placed a set of underpinnings and silk stockings still wrapped in their crinkly tissue atop the dress. Shoes were next, and Phee selected the velvet slippers she'd so hastily shed her first evening here. In a small box she found in the dresser, Phee placed a pair of gold earrings, and an intricate hair fork that displayed a bronzed fern design when secured at the top of her crown and glory.

Surrounded by all the oddities of her aunt's home, Phee had finally found a peace. Even the occasional candle extinguishing itself when she lit it, as though someone behind her had blown it out, no longer unnerved her as much as it had. In some circles, folk would have called Auntie a witch, but there is a different kind of magic that comes over a person when they are content in themselves. They are a silent presence, an impenetrable force that radiates so strongly it calls others.

Phee loved this house. She was safe here. In fact, she was mistress here. What choices and decisions she made were carried out. Phee breathed deeply, inhaling the scent of dusting powder and the ghost of liniment. She touched the neat pile of clothing, ready for Cross's arrival. Soon, this would all be over and she would have to go back to Rosemount, back to her life, and she was loath to do so.

The freedom she felt here was heady, like having too much of Pop's special Engine Fuel punch. One cup of it and Phee was weaving on her feet, almost misjudging the distance to the couch before she collapsed onto the cushions. No, it was more like his spiced rum, a warming sensation that spread throughout her entire being, rounding off the sharp edges of her nervous tension. Either way, it was a drug she quickly became used to, and the thought of it going away was enough to give her tremors.

The settin' up would be on the ninth night. Cross had assured her he would be able to have his part of the proceedings completed by then. After, the burial. And after that, Phee could possibly stretch an extra few days, maybe more, for sorting Auntie's things and any other final duties. Then she could return to a family that constantly wondered when she was going to do something with herself.

"Well, I will enjoy the last of my time here while I can."

Phee left her aunt's bedroom, headed for the stairs. At the top, she paused. Had that been—

Phee turned around to find the door, the one without any visible way of opening it, now stood ajar. She stared at it for long moments as freezing-cold air leeched from beyond it. When she had stood here the first time, the need to enter had been so strong, she'd . . . Phee swallowed, finding her lapse of memory almost more disturbing than her pummeling fruitlessly at the door. She'd needed to get inside so badly at that moment. Why was she so afraid now that it welcomed her? She pulled the shawl closer, against the chill and against her own trepidation. Her mind turned like a wheel, pondering and pondering and coming to the same conclusion each time.

The door is open.

It wasn't before.

It's open now.

Terrified, she thought of closing it again. Forgetting that it existed with its unknowable way of opening and the cold, cold vapor it emitted. But she knew that was impossible. Even without realizing it, she'd drawn closer to the door. Her hand reaching out to feel its solidity, to reassure herself that she hadn't, in fact, fallen into a dream from which she could not wake. It was a real thing, the door. And what was behind it, would that also be real?

She gave in to the curiosity, to the lure of the door and its secrets, and stepped inside, her every breath spurling out in front of her in a vapor.

The room beyond the door was like none she had ever seen. Colder than an icebox, it was the color of spilled wine soaked into wood, this room. From the chandelier in the middle of the ceiling, a drape of sheer fabric descended, split into four parts and attached at each corner with something she could not see. At the center of the room stood a catafalque with a body lain upon it in repose.

Auntie.

A woman stood next to the body, her back to Phee.

Phee's mind hitched, unable to function, to understand how the scene in front of her was true. How did this woman get in the house without Phee's knowledge? How did she get inside this room? How long had she been in here?

Memories rushed back to Phee, the night she had been so tired that she fell against the pillows of her aunt's bed and slept like the dead. She wouldn't have heard anything that night. Or maybe it had happened when she went out to visit Cross. She hadn't left the house otherwise. No windows were in this room, but the light from the ceiling was enough for Phee to see clearly. No shadows crawled here. No mirrors to reflect anything. It was the three of them together in this room: Phee, Auntie Cleo, and this woman.

The woman turned around.

Two, Phee corrected herself. It was the two of them together in this room.

"You found me," Auntie Cleo said. "I knew you would."

Phee's mouth opened, closed, opened again. "You are not dead."

"But I am." Only then did Phee see the transparency of her face and note that no vapor of breath unfurled in front of her mouth as she spoke. The dark walls and fabric-softened light had disguised it well.

"Oh," was all Phee could think of to say.

The two women stood gazing at each other until with a sob, Phee strode forward and threw herself into her aunt's arms. A rush of chill air embraced her, pressing into her back and shoulders, but she didn't pull away.

"No one else would have accepted the pomp. No one from the family. But you might have wanted—"

"Shh . . . I know. No one but you. You were the one I wanted all along."

Worry fell away at Aunt Cleo's words. Phee had been so afraid that after all these years away, her aunt would deem someone else the best person to look after her in death. The dam broken, Phee babbled in her relief. "I had to come . . . I'm sorry I didn't before. When I should have. This time, I just told Mama I was coming and blast what she said." Her words, soaked in tears, came to a halt.

"Your mother always felt I was trying to take you away from her. I suppose in the end, I did."

"She should have forgiven you. They all should have. I'm sorry. I should never have looked in your bag."

Auntie Cleo's spirit held Phee away from her and gazed into her face. The absence of color in her eyes was unnerving, but Phee didn't look away. "No. I loved your curiosity. It inspired me to create this place. When you are a part of something and you're thrown out, so many try to return. I couldn't bring myself to do that. I found another way."

Phee swallowed hard. "How did you do it? Survive on your own?"

Auntie's sigh was long and her form faded for a moment before she became solid once more. "Floodwaters. It was hard to leave them. This place was dry when I arrived and I didn't understand how to live here. I cried a river and the sea came to find out what had caused such an overflow. It

said, 'I just came to see whose tears was saltier than me.'"
Auntie Cleo chuckled.

"It told me it would be all right. How could I leave this place when the whole of the ocean came to see about me? It'll take all your life building something up if you don't get help. It wanted a year of my life to leave something of itself behind. And it kept up its side of the bargain. The little ocean borders the town, joined up with my tear river. Leaving the waters here full of life itself, full of its own creatures."

"And everything else?"

"The sea was first, but they all came to me as I was: weary and sad. The woods, the sky, the marsh, the birds . . . They each wanted a year of my life to create this place and I gave it, so no one else would have to feel the pain I did. The pain of not having a home. I wanted everyone to have a place to go, even if it wasn't the place they came from."

Auntie Cleo looked at herself on the bed, serene, her arms crossed over an envelope. She turned those eyes back to Phee. "And now you also have a place."

She began to fade.

"Wait! I needed to—"

"I'm not going anywhere yet. I just can't hold on to a shape like you can anymore." Auntie Cleo's voice lightened to a whisper, but Phee heard her clearly. "I am here, for as long as you need me."

Take it.

It was the voice Phee had heard her first night here as

she gazed into the mirror and her aunt's room had faded to mist around her. She knew now what those words meant, whispered to her by a woman who understood them more than anyone else she knew.

Take it.

It meant take a risk, take her freedom, take her chance at happiness.

It's yours.

Phee approached her aunt's body, touched the cool skin on the back of her hand with reverence before slipping the envelope free. She sat next to the bed and read each paper through, twice.

It was hers. All of it.

FOURTEEN

It was Phee's ninth night in Auntie Cleo's house and all was ready. Phee walked into the front room and over to the bier holding the sweetgrass casket that contained her aunt's body. Cross had done a perfect job of cosseting her; she looked as though she were sleeping and a gentle nudge would bring a small, drowsy smile to her face.

These past several days with Cross and Aunt Cleo's spirit had been an education: deciding what her aunt would wear, her makeup, her hairstyle, even the casket lining brought up an array of choices. Now all of those decisions had been made, with Cross's gentle guidance and a receipt she'd found in her aunt's things naming the plot she'd purchased for her final resting place. She had even visited Zaye to ask for her assistance in the final acts of care. The woman's dark, liquid eyes had widened at the request, but after a brief hesitation, she'd stamped her foot and agreed.

All together, the three of them prepared Aunt Cleo and her home. The conversation she'd had with Aunt Cleo's spirit had reassured Phee that her choices would be well accepted. All her aunt had wanted was a reconnection with her, and to know that in death, she would not be forgotten. Phee was more than pleased to provide that for her. Tonight was the finale of the entire experience: the settin' up.

Phee held Zaye's hands in her own. "You will sit up with me, won't you?"

But the older woman shook her head and huffed. "No, I cannot. But I will come to visit and pay my respects to my friend."

"Oh, you must!"

"No, *you* must. This is your time, and besides—" She glanced at Cross, placing the final touches on Aunt Cleo's gown before closing the lid. "—you will have company this evening, and far be it from me to play the fifth wheel on the carriage."

During the embrace that followed, Phee felt Zaye's breath on her cheek, warm huffs of air blown through her nose. "Cleo made the right decision in choosing you. Oh, don't look surprised." She chuckled. "Yes, I knew she wanted you to pomp for her. And she knew you would come. She always knew." With those words, Zaye left them, promising to return.

All the planning and details that had her losing sleep and tossing restlessly as she lay in the four-poster rice bed in Aunt Cleo's room had led to this. She would sit up through the night next to her aunt's body in her casket, and receive any guests who wanted to pay their last respects.

Cross had placed Aunt Cleo at the rear of the sitting room before he left to rest up and change clothes. A sprawling, deep green cinnamon fern draped across the bottom of the closed casket lid. The house was dusted, the furniture polished with her aunt's handmade wood cream. All dirty clothes washed, all trash emptied. Phee was tired—oh, so tired—but it was the fatigue of accomplishment, where she could look around and see her own handiwork.

She took a deep breath, taking in the clean scent of pine and evergreen, and knew her aunt would be pleased. Trembling, she reached out and placed her fingers in the prints of those pressed into the handmade brick, feeling the efforts of those who had come before her. Their need to make something that was their own when their dreams had been snatched from under them fairly pulsed from the crushed oystershell and ash. Aunt Cleo had made something here, not just a life for herself, but a space for others without understanding, without acceptance, without a place to rest and see their future on the horizon. This tiny speck of a town, not on any map, was a way station in the world of so many. Maybe those people were not able to be here in body, but their spirits, their lives lived would always reflect this place of solace and succor.

While Phee was too weary for tears now, she knew one day they would come. One day, perhaps months from now, or even a year, she would break down and cry. It would be because of some small item. A trinket that would cause the rising up of all the memories she had set aside in order to give her aunt this send-off. An earring or a faintly fragranced letter. Then she would cry. Great, wrenching sobs for the loss of a woman who had been denied the comfort of family while mired in her own grief. Who had everything taken from her because of a poor choice and had to begin again. For a young girl who had only wanted to please her mother and, in so doing, lost an aunt.

Choice. It came down to that in the end, really. The choices we make, the chances we have. Some of us have too little to make a life yet still manage it somehow. Others have so much and still . . . still. One day the tears would come, Phee knew. Too much hurt had flowed through this family for too many years for her eyes to stay dry. But today was not the day. She still had much to face.

Phee wore her black dress, braided her hair up and away from her face, then placed one of the wingback chairs from near the fireplace at the head of the casket, facing the open front door. Since the parade of funeral directors had left on her first full day here, the sounds of settling and creaking in the otherwise silent house had ceased making her uneasy.

She padded over to the door and glanced outside. The moon rose over the town, creating a thin mist that hovered near the ground as the night cooled. In the distance, she saw Cross walking toward the house, and she waited, leaning against the doorjamb to watch him approach.

"Hail, Phaedra," he said, ascending the steps to the porch and filling the night with the fragrance of his cologne. "Is everything ready for the evening?"

"All except me." She chuckled, and rubbed her arms to smooth the goose bumps forming. "But I'm sure I can do this." Mama would not win; the thought of her gloating was enough to steel Phee's resolve.

Moonlight glinted off the deep hollows of his cheeks, throwing part of his face into shadow. "Would you like me to set up with you?"

His official place was in the background. A support, if an invisible one, should she need a handkerchief, or food, or drink, or in the unlikely event someone needed escorting from the property. But she found his offer to sit next to her welcome. "Please," Phee replied, more grateful than she wanted to admit.

She brought out the bottle of agricole and two of her aunt's crystal lowball glasses while Cross pulled up a matching chair on the opposite end of the coffin, at her aunt's feet, flanking her. She poured a finger into each glass, offered him one, which he tasted appreciatively and complimented.

Phee sipped at the spirit, let it warm a path down her throat to her belly. She leaned back in the seat, letting the alcohol loosen her muscles and her tongue.

"It was a gift from my father."

"And you are sharing it with me. Also, a gift." He removed the fern, lifted the lid of the casket, exposing her aunt to the pleasantly cool, sweet night air. Then he draped his long, spare frame into the chair, crossed one leg over the other, the gleam on his patent leather shoes reflecting the moonlight.

Phee looked at her aunt, so peaceful in repose, and wondered how long she had thought of who would plan her homegoing service. How long she'd known her time was approaching. How difficult it must have been . . . not knowing if someone would ever find and carry out your wishes. Had she hoped Mama would relent and do it, thereby ending their alienation? Auntie Cleo wasn't that naïve. Phee dragged her gaze away, instead staring at the likeness of the moon's face in the shiny surface of Cross's polished shoe.

"They didn't want me to come here and do this, you know. My parents."

When he didn't reply, she looked up to see him watching her. Waiting. The entire town seemed to be waiting.

"I accepted this pomp to prove to myself I could do something without their help. That I could be like Auntie and go my own way."

"And you've done that."

She shook her head. Took a sip of the spirit and tilted her head back, allowing it to slip down her throat without effort. "I haven't done anything except choose you to lay her to rest."

"You *chose* to come here. Of every single body that presented themselves, you chose me." He poured them both another few fingers. "Don't dismiss the importance of choosing."

Phee had no response to that. She rubbed her toes on the polished hardwood, thinking of nothing and everything. "No one is coming to view a body this late."

The moon had moved enough through the inky night to throw shadows that brought Cross's prominent cheekbones into high relief. His eyes were deep, cavernous. "And yet, we wait."

She groaned. "I know this is how it's done and all, but why—"

The words died in her throat at the sound of hoofbeats ringing, covering the cicada song. A rider. Or a carriage, like the one that brought her to Aunt Cleo's in the first place. Phee held her breath while her mind whirled, fighting for what she would say to this visitor who braved the darkest hours to pay respect.

But no rider appeared. A glistening bay horse with a braided mane whose coat smelled of hair pomade entered, appearing through the deepening mists, its head lowered. Phee was stunned into immobility, and could only watch while the beautiful creature nodded to her, then to Cross. It stomped its foreleg, then huffed out a breath through its nostrils.

"Zaye?" Phee whispered, recognizing the woman's actions in the animal. She wondered if this was why she'd been able to carry such weighty packages so easily.

The horse dipped its head in acknowledgment before approaching the casket and pressing its muzzle to her aunt's temple. Phee felt the prod on her own skin. What kind of magic was at play here? Startled, she looked to Cross, and her lips parted on a gasp that never emerged.

Cross's dark gaze was sobering; it spoke the volumes her parents never had. Words of reflection on a life lost, one Phee had never truly gotten to know, and now the library of knowledge, of stories, of her aunt's own personal tale of survival and triumph was closed forever. How the occasion of that loss must be marked and those grieving must be given the time to say their last. Phee inclined her head, understanding within that gaze this was only the beginning of the visitations. The start of a magic that transformed and lingered, not in any elaborate way, but in the small, daily ways that made a life outstanding. Magic had not impressed her in New Charleston, but here in Horizon, it changed people, infusing them with subtle strength, enough to allow them to carry on.

More hoofbeats arrived some minutes after the first visitor. At least Phee felt like it was minutes. Time once again had ceased to move around her. It no longer felt real, sitting up with Cross, her aunt between them like a chaperone. The open front door glowed like a portal to another world, with moonlight, and perhaps even with magic. Anything, Phee knew, could happen now. She felt drunk not only with her father's smoky spirits, but also with the ones arriving.

A buzzard whose shaggy feathers reminded her of the coat Ol' Miss Johnson wore when she'd met her on the street strutted in. The hunchbacked bird gave Phee a cursory yet assessing glance, then loped in a circle around the casket, then flew away after dropping a handkerchief at its base. Phee nodded to herself. The Cooks' assessment of the woman as surly had been right, but she had come all the same.

"Miss. Brer Cross," a six-point buck addressed Phee and her companion. He had arrived some while after a soft-eyed roe deer and a spotted fawn who left as silently as they entered. He approached the casket much as the others had, but did not touch her aunt. Instead, he inclined his great head. His eyes were glassy with disbelief.

"You done dig grave?" he asked of Cross.

"No, brer." The mortician's voice was long-suffering. He glanced at Phee with an expression she couldn't read. "Not yet."

The buck touched his antlers to the casket twice, the sound hollow. "Still time, then, missus." Slowly, he backed away, then turned and clomped out of the house.

"Time for what?"

Cross swirled the liquid, then held it up to an eye. "For final goodbyes." He downed the rest of the drink.

Any further questions Phee may have had were silenced within the translucent mist of magic drifting into the house. A reverent hush, not only from her, but from Cross and from the night itself. The tonal hum of cicada song vibrated within her chest, and in a rush of awareness, Phee felt a presence alongside her. Unlike before—in the mirror, in the bath—it waited without eagerness. Perhaps even time itself waited now, too.

A sloshing of water joined the dirge. The ocean tide rose and entered the room, bringing its children of fin and scale and shell. Phee felt its seeking pressure, kitten-curious around her bare feet and ankles. Strange there was no other sensation of wet or heat or cold from it, only the briny scent of life within its waves.

"Is she resting with me?" it asked after greeting Phee,

the voice an undulating ebb and flow from baritone to alto and back again.

"Not this one," Cross replied.

To Phee's surprise, the sea bubbled, amused. "In the end, all will be mine, you know."

"We know no such thing." Phee's companion waved one hand dismissively, while raising his empty glass with the other in a parody of a toast.

A wave lifted, climbing the casket stand, and pulled itself up to peer inside. "I see . . . Well, I just came to hail." With more reverence, it retreated with its offspring, leaving dry floorboards dusted with a powdery layer of salt.

Aunt Cleo, even without the support of her family, had endured, persevered, and thrived. Had created a place for others to do the same. The visitors tonight had shown her what impact she'd had. Despite Mama, despite it all. Maybe Phee could do the same.

Cross seemed to know the events of the night had profoundly impacted Phee and she needed to be on her own to digest them.

"One more," he said, looking to the door. "I hope. There is still time."

The sky had only begun to lighten from the deepest part of the night when footsteps approached the door. Through the mists came a familiar figure.

"Daddy!" Phee made to stand up, but his look of concern and confusion made her hesitate. The presence from before pressed tenderly down onto her shoulders and she kept her seat.

Phenton made no move to acknowledge his daughter as he walked toward the casket, but under the moonlight, Phee thought she saw his jaw tighten. For long moments, he stood in front of it, looking down into her aunt's serene face. He swallowed hard before he spoke.

"I didn't want to come here, Cleo. Not once my baby girl said she was going to set with you, but here I am. And we both know why, don't we?"

The hush from the earlier visits had gone, giving way to a thrum of weighted electricity that left a sweet, pungent scent of ozone-laden storm building in the room.

"If no one noticed that necklace missing, none of this would have happened. I had already taken it to the jewelers and got the certificate of valuation that would be the collateral for the surety loan. If I'd had just five more minutes, I could have put it back where it was and Maddie would never have been the wiser." He rocked back and forth on his heels as if to soothe himself. "But Phee always noticed. I should've thought about that."

Phee gasped, covered her mouth with her hand. She'd been so young that the details of the night the family ousted Aunt Cleo were blurred. The memory returned to her with a jolt of shock. She had pointed out to Mama that the necklace—a cameo of a woman's profile rendered in onyx, silhouetted against a buffed oyster-hued background—was no longer tucked under Gran's wide lace collar.

"I just needed the money. I would have replaced it as soon as the next batch of rum sold. It needed longer aging and I hadn't planned—" He stopped, rubbed a hand roughly over his face. "You know Maddie better than anyone. When she gets the scent of something wrong, she never lets go until she finds out."

After a few tension-wrapped moments of silence in the room where Phee could hear her heart beating inside her chest and the swirl of her own blood through her veins drowned out her father's shaky breaths, Phenton continued.

"Maddie and I were married, and we had Phee. You didn't have anyone . . . I just figured if somebody had to . . ." Phenton's tears fell onto the casket, lay like diamonds on its edge. "I couldn't let my baby girl grow up without me."

For the first time that night, Phee felt icy cold encircle her. Not from the heavy mist in the room, but from within. This . . . all of this was *his fault*. The words echoed in her mind. His fault Aunt Cleo left, his fault the family turned their backs, his fault she was even here now.

Another word sprang up to replace the echo. *Choice*. Phee had taken control of her own mind and made the choice to be here for Aunt Cleo. Her parents had nothing to do with her decision, and for that she was grateful. Of her own accord, she had stepped up to give the exiled woman her rightful send-off. A smile tugged at her cheeks, widening to a full, unladylike grin. A gentle squeeze on her shoulders, the passing breath against her cheek like a kiss, and the presence was gone.

Her father stood at the casket, openly weeping now. Phee's heart was in pieces: part of it aching for his pain, part of it full of tenderness for her aunt's life away from her family, and yet another part full of righteous anger that her father hadn't brought her mother along to witness his confession. Still, her heart beat strongly, swollen with the magic of spirits.

"It's almost morning." Cross stood, gently led her father away from the casket, and closed the lid. He draped the fern over it once again, then made a beckoning motion with one arm, and the entire casket lifted from its stand. "Her spirit is pleased, and we must depart this place."

With that declaration, Cross walked out the front door, now glowing pink with rising daylight, and the casket followed him.

Phee rose from the chair, fortified by her success and the agricole swirling through her. After donning her slippers, she too followed Cross. Her father came along; she could hear his footsteps, but she didn't turn to look at him, didn't speak to him. His secret, revealed after all those years, was something to address at a later date. Address it she would, because she refused to leave it to fester like the heirloom cameo Mama decided not to bury with Gran. The cameo Mama never even wore. But this wasn't the time.

The procession shadowing Cross included the spirit residents of the town who had come to visit during the night, all of them reverent and whisper-draped as they marched through the streets toward a set of gates in the distance. At their approach, the gates opened in welcome. Cross gestured and the layers of soil rolled back like carpet to expose a hole in the earth. Phee was reminded of the graveyard jar she'd found in the kitchen and wondered if that was in itself her instruction. The casket lowered into the ground while Phee spoke a few words through the tightness in her throat before nodding to Cross that he could close over the burial plot. Once it was done, she poured out the last of the bottle and nestled the glass into the ground.

She would never remember what she said, but as the sun rose and the visitors returned to wherever spirits reside, she was left with a sense of peace and right. Most of all, she was left with the sense that her aunt was pleased. When Cross confirmed her suspicions, Phee didn't ask how he knew.

He turned those deep, cavernous eyes on her. "My deepest sympathies to you, Phee."

She thanked him, feeling a satisfaction she hadn't felt in perhaps ever. "This may be an inappropriate time, but would you be interested in having an assistant?"

His lips curved in that tender almost-smile that had become so familiar. "Perhaps a partner. We can discuss after sunfall, if you like. I make a good scripture cake."

"I'll see you this evening, then." Phee smiled until he faded into the rising sunlight.

"I'm so sorry, Sugarfoot."

Phee started; she'd purposefully ignored her father during her eulogy and the interment, hoping he would leave her to finish this on her own. Instead, he'd waited for her at the edge of the cemetery.

"How did you even get here? Does Mama know where you are?"

"I hired a mud wagon."

Phee frowned. Mud wagons were used for rough terrain; it was quick, but hard travel usually reserved for deliveries. He'd been desperate to get here in time. Once he'd decided to come, that was.

"And?" she pressed.

He turned away from her direct gaze, falling back into his usual habit of saying little, and hoping to escape unscathed.

"Does she know you're here, Pop?"

"No, your mother is sleeping." He paused. "I let her test my newest batch of rum."

It seemed her father was no stranger to his own manner of hexing. She made no reply, but started back down the path through the gates and out of the graveyard. She still thought of the house as her aunt's, probably a part of her always would, but she had a piece of paper that said it belonged to her now.

"But when we get back home," he continued, matching her stride easily, "I'll make it up to you."

"How?"

"You can have the bookkeeping job at the distillery. I'll make it full time. I'll tell your mother you can do the job. She'll leave you alone."

Phee nodded, stepping high through the long grasses. While the floodwaters from the sea's visit had receded, the ground was still soaked as thoroughly as a milk cake. The fog of the night had lifted, and the morning sun was rising, promising a bright warmth that she was looking forward to indulging in.

"But will you tell Mama what you did?" she asked.

He stammered a flurry of words that in the end said nothing.

"Why not?" she asked.

"I don't see the point, Phaedra." He was irritated now. "Your aunt's gone and I've made peace with what I did. All speaking on it's going to do is get your mother riled up and angry."

"Even if she gets angry, she deserves to know, Pop! Stop being afraid of her anger, and stop treating her like a child."

Her father waved his hand dismissively. "I don't treat her like a child."

"Oh yes, you do. Like a spoiled child who has everything she wants until she gets out of hand and you then correct her. But with the things that truly matter, you don't trust her. She doesn't get enough information from you to make any choices for herself. Only for me."

"But that's—"

It was Phee's turn to wave away his response. "I, for one, believe she should be furious at you, because you deserve every moment of that fury. You left her with the belief Aunt Cleo had duped her, when it was her own husband all along."

A deep breath in through her nose, out through pursed lips. Maybe Aunt Cleo had forgiven him, but she wasn't ready to. "Did you even know that Gran named Aunt Cleo as her pomp? How Mama managed to get that honor for herself, I haven't the foggiest. But you two seem made for each other. Maybe you can discuss your deceptions over tea and cakes."

He opened his mouth, but Phee wasn't finished yet.

"Ten years, Pop. Ten. Whole. Years," she said, alighting the steps to the little house that had welcomed her into its mysteries at a time when she had been so unsure of herself and what she wanted from her life. It called softly, soothing the ire that rose at her father's betrayal and the secrets her family had kept for a decade. Today would be a good day to spend inside, soaking in whatever magic still lingered in those walls.

Phenton St. Margaret stood at the foot of the steps, shaking his head.

The door swung open at Phee's touch. "I'll be staying here for a while, and I'll send for my things."

"What do I say to your mother? If you don't come home, she'll never let this go until she discovers what happened." He rubbed his hand over his lower jaw, his gaze darting around before he hurriedly ascended the steps to stand next to her. "Please see sense. What do you expect me to do?"

Phee almost felt sorry for him, but his choices had brought him to this crossroads. As had her mother's. As had her own. The difference was: she was pleased with hers.

"I don't know, Pop. But I have company coming and I need to tidy up."

He glared at her, his eyes shimmering with unshed tears. His jaw worked back and forth as if he was trying to hold back a demand he knew he had no right to make. "You don't understand—"

"On the contrary," she said, closing the door in his face.

She didn't wait to hear his footsteps retreat. He would depart in his own time. Instead she drew open all of the curtains in the house—*her* house, she reminded herself—and pulled the shawl closer over her shoulders. Phee had upheld her promise to herself. She had left Rosemount on her own terms, assisted in a corpse easing, and laid her aunt to rest in a manner befitting someone who was loved. The true lesson she had learned was to trust herself, her instincts, and her intuition. The cozy house, the overgrown garden, the offer of employment—it was enough to make a life. A good life. It had been for her aunt. Phee had even changed her mind about burying Aunt Cleo in the shawl, deciding her aunt's words of "Take it for yourself" extended to the garment she had come to love.

Phee retrieved the unfinished needlework from the office drawer, then continued to the kitchen. There, she set out dessert plates and forks for her company that evening and lit the stove. She left the curtains parted and the windows cracked open all day to show Aunt Cleo the way to eternity, but her aunt would leave in her own time.

Until then, Phee had much to occupy her. There was the possibility of the partnership with Cross, as he had mentioned her natural affinity for the dead. However, her primary focus would be to continue the work her aunt had started. Phee didn't want any more people to experience Elijah's fate. And so she would carry on the duty of letting every lost soul know that if they needed a place where they were welcome, they could look to Horizon.

ACKNOWLEDGMENTS

Bringing a book into the world is an enormous feat of energy, effort, and, in some cases, the stars aligning. *Psychopomp & Circumstance* wouldn't have been possible without the help, encouragement, and talents of a number of people. Omission of anyone is my oversight, and please know I still appreciate you.

I'd like to mention:

My grandmother, whose homegoing I planned more than a decade ago—with her instructions. It was my closest experience with the final care of a loved one and may have planted the seed for this story.

My mom, for all you've sacrificed and all you've taught me. And for supporting my love of books from the beginning.

My husband for being the most amazing, loving, and supportive man I've ever known.

My father, whose homegoing I planned while also working on the final edits for this book.

DaVaun: for seeing the beauty in an early draft this

story and for your thoughtful edits. I'm honored by your support of my work.

The writers who beta read this story in one version or another: Ronnie, Wendi, Celeste, Kirk, Brent, Eboni, Teri, Greg, Luwana, and Tony. Thank you for your feedback and insights. I truly value all of you and your creativity is boundless. I'm honored to be your contemporary.

Those who provided such wonderful early blurbs: Moniquill, Claire, Nicole, and A$iah. It meant so much that you took the time to read my work.

As always, to my feline writing companions, Samurai and Loki, who were there waiting when I emerged from the pages.

And finally:

My thanks to you, reader, for reading.

ABOUT THE AUTHOR

The Aneris Collective, LLC

EDEN ROYCE is a writer from Charleston, South Carolina, now living in South East England. She is a Shirley Jackson Award finalist and a Bram Stoker Award nominee for her adult fiction, which has appeared in a variety of print and online publications. Her books for young readers have won multiple awards, including the Ignyte Award, the Bram Stoker Award, and the Walter Dean Myers Honor.